Curious George's

BIG BOOK

of

DISCOVERY

Clarion Books

*An Imprint of HarperCollins**Publishers***

Boston   New York

ISBN: 978-1-328-85712-5

clarionbooks.com
curiousgeorge.com

Manufactured in China
22 SCP 10 9 8 7 6 5 4 3 2

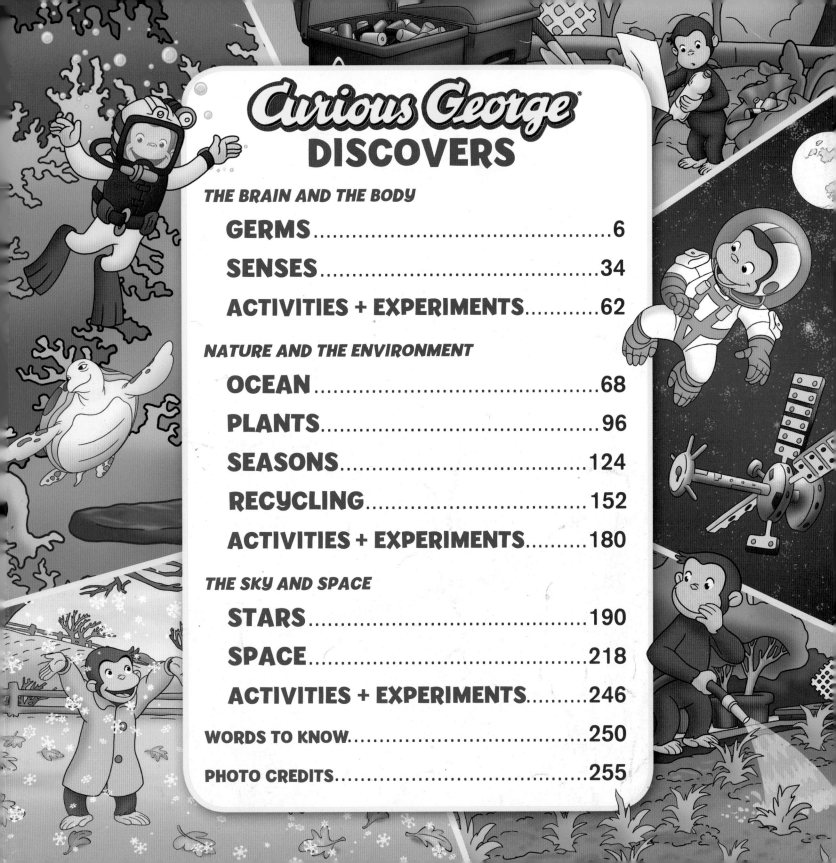

Curious George® DISCOVERS

THE BRAIN AND THE BODY

GERMS...6

SENSES...34

ACTIVITIES + EXPERIMENTS............62

NATURE AND THE ENVIRONMENT

OCEAN...68

PLANTS...96

SEASONS..124

RECYCLING...152

ACTIVITIES + EXPERIMENTS............180

THE SKY AND SPACE

STARS...190

SPACE...218

ACTIVITIES + EXPERIMENTS............246

WORDS TO KNOW.................................250

PHOTO CREDITS...................................255

THE BRAIN AND THE BODY

Your body has many different parts inside and out. Did you know that your brain is located inside your head and protected by a skull? The brain is the boss of your body—it controls everything you do or feel. Isn't that incredible? There are lots of things about our bodies that we all have in common—a beating heart, lungs that make us breathe, two eyes, two ears, one nose, one mouth—but lots that make us different, too, like the color of our hair, skin, and eyes, or how tall or short we are. Are you curious about all the amazing things that go on in your brain and body? So is George!

In this section, you'll learn about:

GERMS AND BACTERIA
WHY WE GET SICK AND HOW TO STAY HEALTHY
THE FIVE SENSES AND HOW THEY WORK TOGETHER
THE IMPORTANCE OF SLEEP

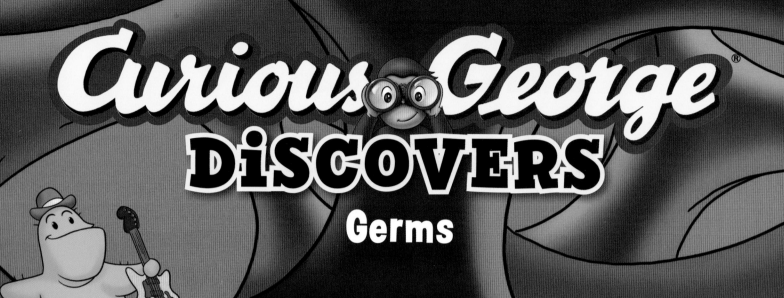

Curious George DISCOVERS

Germs

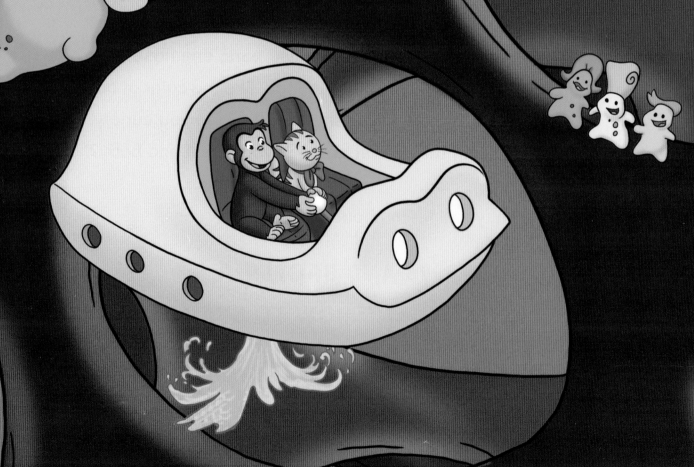

George is a good little monkey, and always very curious. But sometimes even good little monkeys find themselves not feeling so well. How did George know he was sick? The story starts with spaghetti sauce!

George's favorite day of the week was Sauce Day at Chef Pisghetti's restaurant. He always gave Chef Pisghetti some tips to make the best sauce. But today, instead of being able to taste the chef's new Molto Jolto sauce, George couldn't taste anything!

Did you know . . .

when you say you can't taste something because you have a cold, it's really because you can't smell it? Your sense of smell is responsible for most of what you "taste," so when your nose is stuffed up, it's hard to smell or taste much of anything.

Chef Pisghetti sent George home, and the man with the yellow hat sent George to bed. Then, he took George's temperature.

"Fever. Stuffy nose. Clammy paws," said the man. "You are definitely fighting a germ, George."

Do you know what a germ is? George was curious.

Did you know . . .

the word *biology* means the study of life and living things? If you are a biologist you might work with plants, animals, or the human body! Someday you will study biology in school.

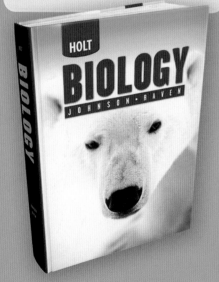

The man got out a book. There was a picture of a funny-looking blob.

"This is a bad germ, George. There are good germs and bad germs. A bad germ is making you sick," the man explained. "Germs are very small. They can be found anywhere in your body: your nose, your mouth, your stomach, your lungs. But that's enough biology for today. Tired monkeys need their rest."

George might have been sick, but he was still curious. Where did the germ come from? And more important, how could he get rid of it? He was still wondering when he dozed off . . .

Soon George was dreaming. In his dream he was very small . . . like a germ! He and his pal Gnocchi were going to take a trip inside George's sleeping body to fight off the bad germs!

Did you know . . .

The man with the yellow hat said that some germs are good and some are bad. That means that in your body right now are some bacteria, or germs, that help your body instead of making you sick. Good germs can help make vitamins that your body needs. You can even get some of these good bacteria by eating favorite foods such as yogurt and cheese!

George and Gnocchi zoomed into sleeping George's mouth and landed right on his tongue. It was soft and squishy. And there was music playing! They hadn't expected that! What could it be? It seemed to be coming from his nose.

When George and Gnocchi got to the nose, they saw a funny-looking blob strumming a guitar and singing!

"I'll make you sniff and I'll make you sneeze.
You won't be smelling that smelly cheese!
We'll be making you sweat and making you squirm,
Because that's how germs are being germs!"

George could hardly believe his eyes.

"I'm Toots, the singing germ," he introduced himself, "and these are my backup singers, the Germettes."

Did you know . . .

when you are sick with a cold germ, the inside of your nose becomes inflamed, or irritated and swollen, and produces mucus that stuffs you up or makes your nose run? Your body makes mucus all the time, but when you are sick there is more of it. Sometimes it helps to use a humidifier, take a hot bath, and drink a lot of fluids.

Seeing Toots in his nose made George upset.
He wanted that germ out of him!

But Toots did not want to go. In fact, he
took the Germettes and headed to George's
lungs, laughing and singing all the way.

George and Gnocchi chased the germs to the lungs. George noticed that when the lungs got smaller, air went out. And when the lungs got bigger, a rush of air came in. He was watching himself breathe!

Test it out!

Put your hand just above your belly button. Take a deep breath in. Do you feel your tummy get bigger? That's because your lungs are filling up with air. Now breathe all the way out. What happens then? Try breathing fast or very slow. See how your body changes when you do this.

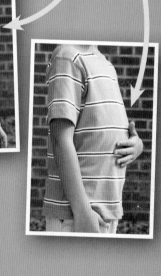

George's lungs gave him an idea. He remembered something he saw in the germ book: coughing and sneezing are the lungs' way of doing their job and trying to force out bad germs. All George had to do was sneeze Toots right out of his body!

Did you know . . .
it is really hard to sneeze with your eyes open? Your body sneezes when it is trying to get something out of your nose—a germ, dust, pet hair, pollen . . . anything! Closing your eyes is just a reflex that your body makes when a sneeze happens, the same as when your doctor tests your reflexes on your knee!

George and Gnocchi chased Toots and the Germettes all the way to George's nose. Then, with one big sneeze (thanks to some well-positioned tickling), out went Toots and the Germettes . . . out into the air, looking for a new place to live.

A few days later, George was feeling much better.
He had taken lots of naps, drunk lots of water and
juice, and sneezed out those germs. He could even smell again! But
it was clear where Toots and the Germettes had found a new home.
George's friend the man with the yellow hat was sick!

The man had taken such good care of George when he was sick. Now George wanted to help his friend get better, too. So he made some soup.

George brought the soup to the man's bed.

"Thanks, George," the man said. But when he tried
the soup, he couldn't taste anything.

George wanted to taste it, but his friend stopped him.

"George, don't use that spoon! It might be covered with my cold germs. You don't want to get sick again, do you?" the man asked.

George definitely did not want to get sick again.

That made George curious. How else did germs get from one person to another? He looked at his germ book. George knew that the germs were in him just a few days ago, but his friend had not used George's spoon — or fork, or cup! Do you think the man caught George's germs when he sneezed or coughed?

Looking at the book made George sleepy. He drifted into another dream — now he and Gnocchi were inside the man with the yellow hat's body. There was that music again, coming from the man's stomach. They needed to find Toots so they could kick him out again!

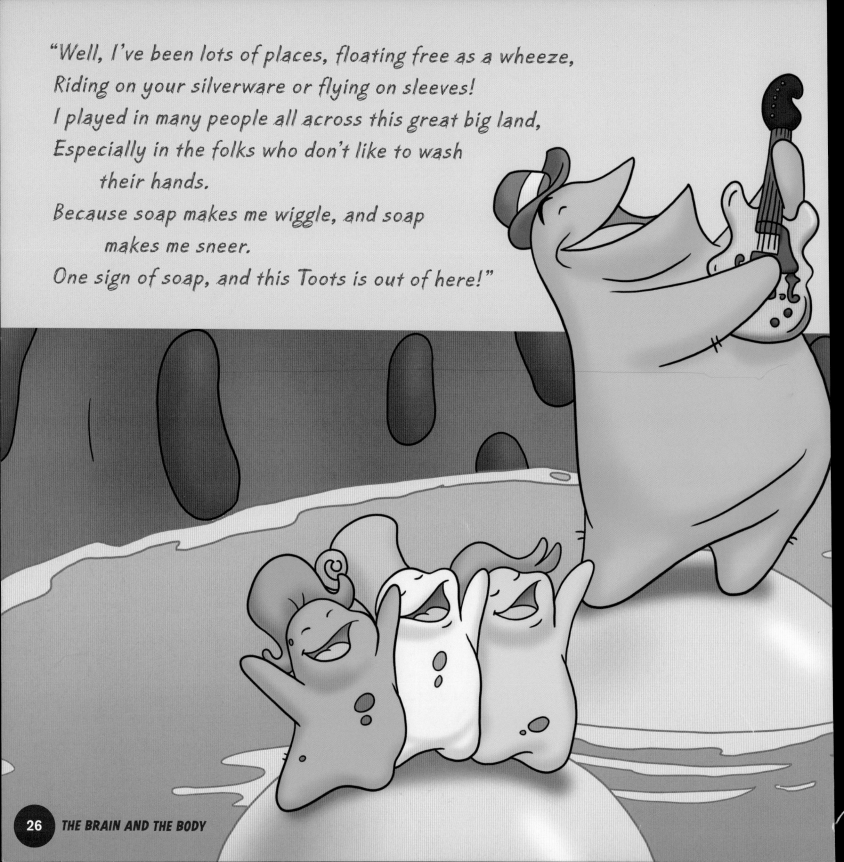

"Well, I've been lots of places, floating free as a wheeze,
Riding on your silverware or flying on sleeves!
I played in many people all across this great big land,
Especially in the folks who don't like to wash
    their hands.
Because soap makes me wiggle, and soap
    makes me sneer.
One sign of soap, and this Toots is out of here!"

If George heard Toots correctly, getting his friend to wash his hands would be a good way to help him get rid of the germs and feel better.

But Toots and the Germettes remembered George, and knew they needed to get away from him. "We're off to play in another body," Toots said — they were going to infect someone else!

Did you know . . .

even though George saw a picture of a germ in a book, germs are invisible to humans? They are so small that you can see them only by looking through a microscope. Germs can hide on just about anything a person touches! So it is important to use healthy habits like using tissues, washing your hands, and staying home from school when you are sick.

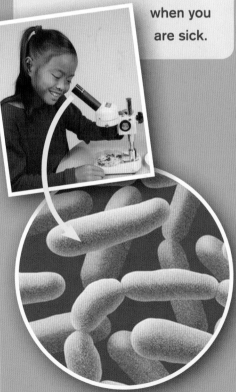

"Get ready to hop on that hand when he wipes his nose!" yelled Toots to his Germettes. George didn't want the germs inside his friend, but he didn't want anyone else to be sick either. He had to stop them.

When the bell rang and the man got up to answer the door, Toots and the Germettes were ready for a new body . . . Professor Wiseman's! She had also made soup for her sick friend.

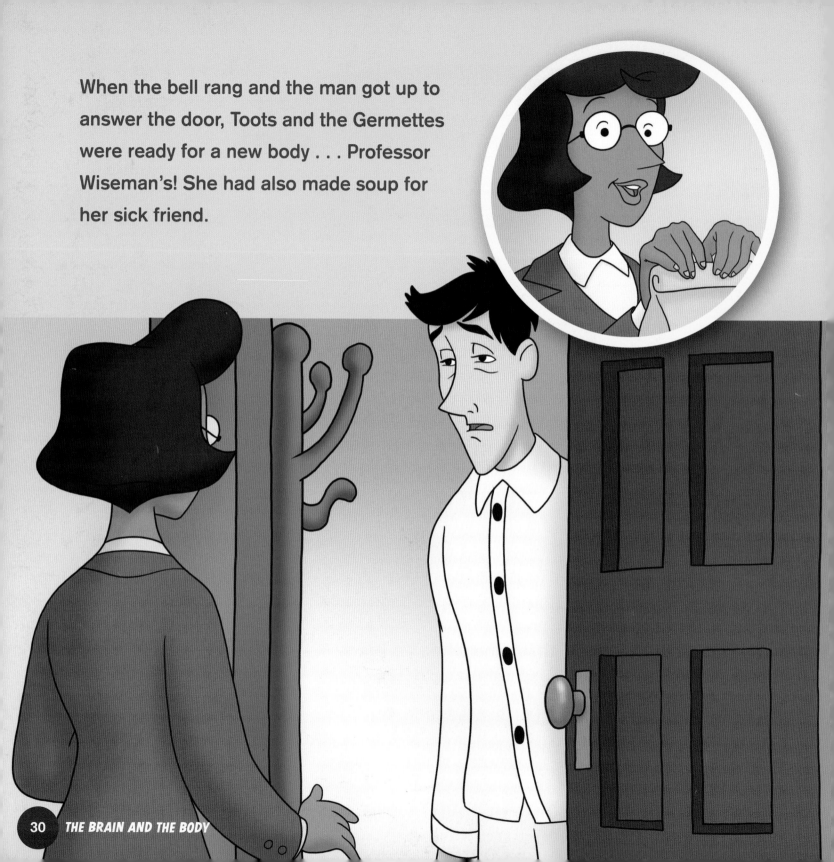

George and Gnocchi zoomed out after the germs and landed with a thud on Professor Wiseman's hand. The germs were startled. "Oooh, it feels like something is crawling on my hands!" Professor Wiseman said. "I should probably wash them inside."

Professor Wiseman went to the bathroom and washed Toots and the Germettes right down the drain!

Not only had George chased those germs out of his friend, he (and some soap) had stopped them from getting Professor Wiseman sick, too.

When George woke up from his dream, he felt great. But he went straight to the bathroom to wash his hands—and feet—just in case. After two icky adventures with Toots, this healthy little monkey wanted to stay that way!

Curious George DISCOVERS

Senses

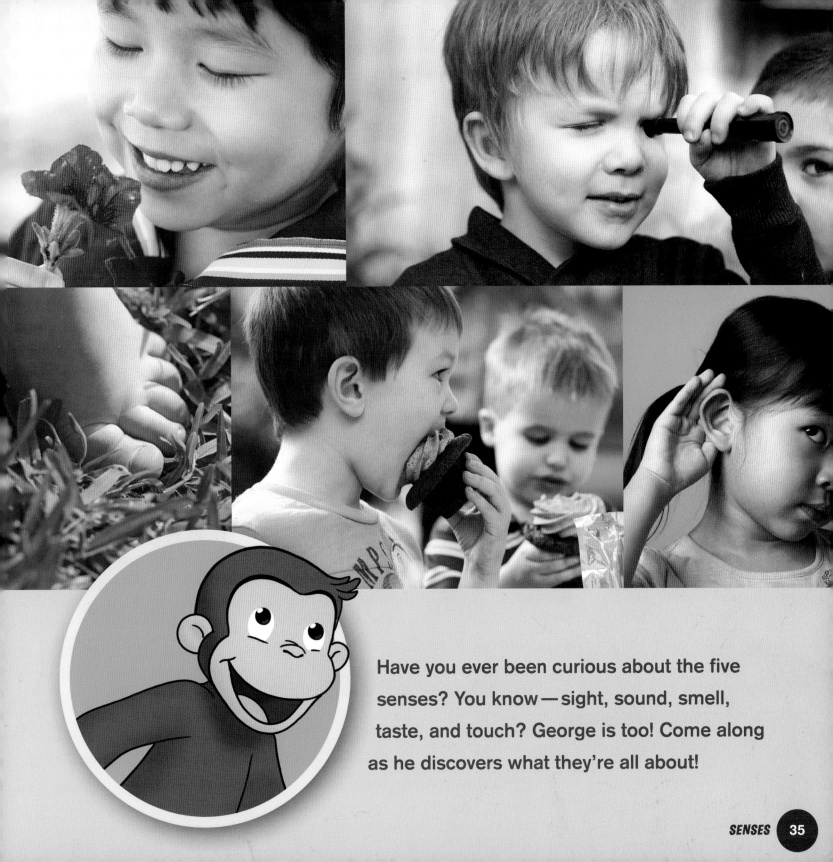

Have you ever been curious about the five senses? You know—sight, sound, smell, taste, and touch? George is too! Come along as he discovers what they're all about!

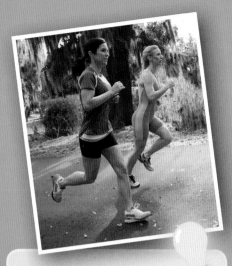

In the country, things moved at a slower pace.
Except for the man with the yellow . . . helmet!
He was training for a triathlon race on Saturday.
George was helping by keeping time.

Did you know . . .

a triathlon is a three-part race made up of swimming, cycling, and running? It takes a lot of time and energy to train for a triathalon. Which part of the race do you think would be the hardest? Which part would you be best at?

While the man was training, the roof of George's house was being repaired. When George and the man got home, the roof repairman told them, "The hole is bigger than we thought. A lot of water got in."

The hole was right above their bedrooms. Until it was fixed, they had to move their beds downstairs into the living room.

George was excited to sleep in the living room.

It would be an adventure!

But George discovered that there are also problems with sleeping somewhere new. Especially after dark! In the dark, everything looked and sounded different. It made it hard for George to sleep.

Did you know...

that sight is what happens when light enters our eyes? Then messages are sent to the brain, which tells us what we see. In a way, our eyes are like tiny cameras. But without light, we can't see anything!

Then something else made it hard for George to sleep — bats! George woke up to the sound of bats screeching in the dark.

Did you know . . .
bats are nocturnal? That means bats are awake at night and sleep during the day. It's easier for them to hunt bugs and avoid predators when it's dark out. There are many nocturnal animals, including owls, mice, and raccoons. Would you rather sleep at night or during the day?

The bats woke the man up too. "They must have come in through the hole in the roof," he said. The man tried to get the bats out of the house, but he tripped over something in the dark. "I wish I were a bat! Then I could get around in the dark too." George was curious.

THE BRAIN AND THE BODY

"Like us, bats can't see very well in the dark. They use their ears instead of eyes," the man explained. "Bats screech to find out where they are. Their voices bounce off of things so they know where things are even if they can't see. They use their sense of sound to hear where they're going."

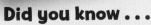

Did you know . . .

the term for how bats find their way around in the dark is echolocation? Bats have the best hearing of all land mammals. They often have huge ears compared to the rest of their body. Bats make sounds and listen for the echoes when their sounds bounce back. Those echoes help them locate nearby objects and figure out how close they are. Another animal that uses echolocation is the dolphin.

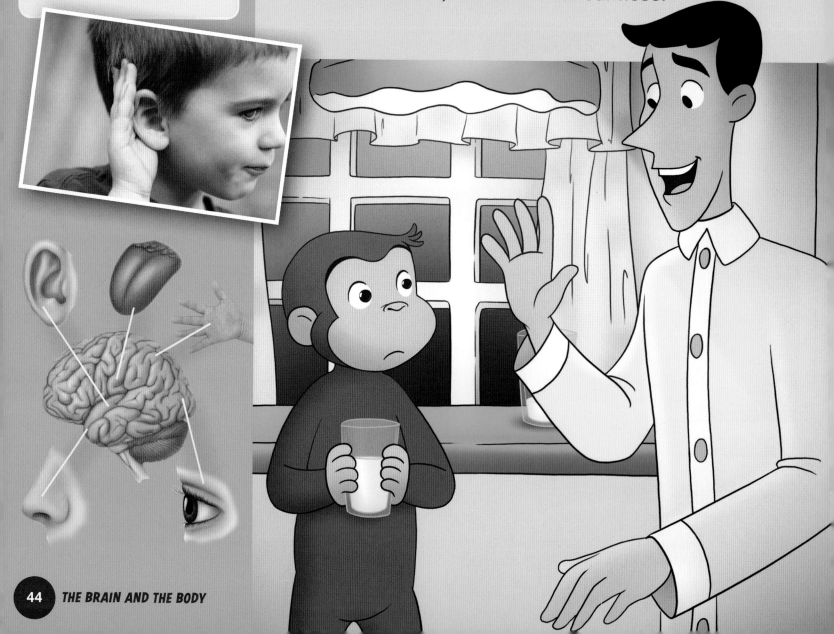

Did you know . . .

that even though we have five different senses, they all work together to collect information and send it to our brain? This gives us a full picture of the world around us.

Once the bats were out of the house, the man gave George a glass of milk to help him sleep. "You remember the five senses, George: sight, sound, taste, touch, and smell! We see with our eyes, hear with our ears, taste with our mouth, touch with our hands and skin, and smell with our nose."

"Do you think you can sleep now, George?" the man asked.

George could. He went right back to sleep.

But the man didn't. The next day, he looked really tired during triathlon training. With the race only two days away, the man needed to get plenty of sleep to help keep his energy up.

George hoped the man would sleep tonight. And he did.
But George was still wide awake! He needed another
glass of milk to help him fall asleep.

George didn't want to wake the man up by turning on the light, so he tried to find his way to the kitchen in the dark. But he kept bumping into things. Then George remembered what the man told him about bats. George thought he could use his voice and his sense of hearing to find his way in the dark too.

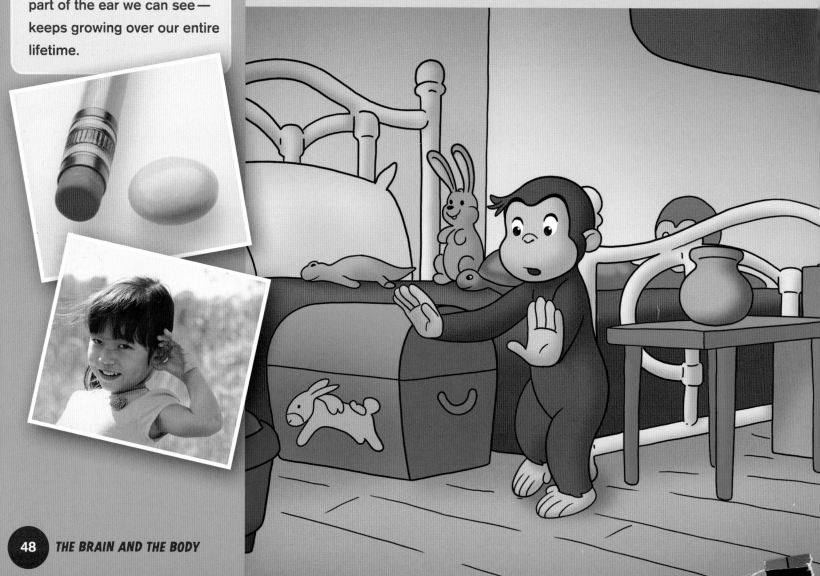

Explore further:

Humans might not be able to hear as well as bats, but we can still use sound to figure out the distance and location of an object. Next time you're outside, close your eyes for a minute. What sounds do you hear? Can you tell where they're coming from? Can you tell if they are close to you or far away?

He tried screeching like a bat, but he couldn't hear his voice bounce off of anything. He tried a little louder . . . and a little louder . . .

"What are you doing?" cried the man. All that screeching had woken him up.

The next day, George felt awful. He'd kept the man up again. If only he had a way to quietly find his way to the kitchen in the dark. He couldn't see or hear his way. Then George got an idea while eating his breakfast—maybe he could taste his way to the kitchen!

George put some oatmeal on the floor. He could use it to make a trail.

"George!" The man cried out to stop him. Eating off the floor is never a good idea! If George couldn't use taste, sight, or sound, what senses were left?

Oatmeal might not belong on the floor, but it does belong in a curious monkey's tummy. George took a deep breath in. It smelled good. If he left the oatmeal out, would he be able to smell his way to the kitchen? Just then, the man came over. "Want some honey with your oatmeal?" he asked George.

The honey was sticky, and that got George thinking. Maybe he could use touch!

George spread a honey path out along the floor. If George felt the honey with his feet, he'd know if he was going the right way. He was so excited about his path, he could hardly wait to try it out.

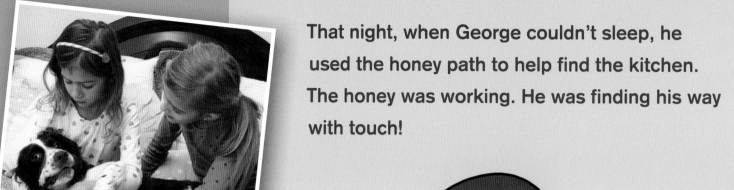

That night, when George couldn't sleep, he used the honey path to help find the kitchen. The honey was working. He was finding his way with touch!

Did you know . . .

that our sense of touch is the first of our senses to develop before we are born? It is the main way we learn about the world around us when we are babies. Touch can also keep us feeling good. Petting a cat or a dog, or giving a hug to a friend or parent, helps us feel happy. Give it a try the next time you need some cheering up!

But now the honey was stuck to George's feet. It was hard to find the path because it felt like the honey was everywhere.

"George? What are you doing?" the man asked.

Oops! George had woken his friend up again.

The next day, George decided to feel his way to the kitchen using something soft, not sticky. George looked in his toy box. Maybe he could use his stuffed animals! George's soft path had to work, because the man's race was tomorrow and he needed to get some sleep.

George's stuffed animals would tell him where the furniture was, but he needed more soft things to lead him to the kitchen. So George rolled up some towels to make a path.

The man was so tired that he went to bed early. George didn't even have to wait until his bedtime to try his soft path out. Using his hands and feet, George worked his way to the kitchen. And he made it all the way without waking his friend up!

That night, George used his path many, many times. Since he was so excited about the man's race tomorrow, George was the one who couldn't sleep.

The next morning, George was there to cheer the man on
as he swam . . . and rode . . . and ran his way to the finish line.
But George missed the finish!

Because all that walking around at night made
a monkey very sleepy.

THERE'S MORE TO EXPLORE ABOUT THE WORLD AROUND US!

Five-Second Rule

If you drop a piece of food on the ground, do you ever hear someone say, "Pick it up, quick! Five-second rule!"? Often, people call out the five-second rule because they think that if you get food off the floor quickly enough, there won't be any germs on it. But did you know that scientists have done studies to show that even in less than five seconds, germs can make their way onto your food and into your body?

Try an experiment at home.

You will need . . .

- **two slices of fresh bread**
- **two zipper-lock bags**
- **a permanent marker**

Directions:
First, wash your hands with soap and water. Place one slice of bread in a bag and close it tight, making sure to get all of the extra air out. Label this bag "A" with your marker.

Drop the other piece of bread flat onto the floor (in your kitchen, bathroom, on a rug, or even outside!). Leave the bread on the ground for five full seconds (count 1 Mississippi, 2 Mississippi . . .). Then place that piece of bread in the second bag. Don't forget to get all of the extra air out and zip it closed tight. Label this bag "B" so you remember which is which.

Check on your pieces of bread each day until mold begins to show. Did one piece get moldy more quickly, or in more places? Which one? What do you think happened?

Healthy Habits

Wash up!

Make a list of times you and your family should wash your hands with soap and water, and post it on your refrigerator or in your bathroom.

Some ideas:

- Before and after eating
- After using the bathroom
- After playing with animals, even your pets!
- Before and after visiting sick friends or family
- After you cough, sneeze, or blow your nose
- After playing outside

You can sing a song to make sure you are washing your hands long enough to get rid of germs. A good one to try is "Happy Birthday"!

An Apple a Day

The old saying "an apple a day keeps the doctor away" may have some truth to it. That doesn't mean you'll never get sick if you eat an apple every day. But an apple has many great nutrients that help keep your body healthy, and eating apples regularly may make you healthier in the long run. Just be sure to eat the skin, too, since that's where most of the nutrients are!

It is always a good idea to eat a variety of fruits, vegetables, and whole grains for a well-balanced diet.

Explore further!

Eating right and washing your hands aren't the only ways to stay healthy (though they are important!).

Here are some ways you can stay healthy all year round:

- Get enough rest (that means 10 hours of sleep a night!)
- Drink plenty of water
- Get lots of fresh air and exercise
- Dress appropriately for all weather
- Take a vitamin
- Visit the doctor regularly

Exploring the Senses:
SIGHT SOUND TASTE TOUCH SMELL

We use our five senses to understand our environment. Our senses work together to send information to our brain, and help us experience what's around us in lots of ways. We're always using at least one of our five senses!

Test it out!

George had to rely on one of his other senses to help him find the kitchen because it was too dark to see. How good are your senses when you can't see?

You will need . . .

- a parent or friend
- several objects from your home
- a blindfold

What to do:

Ask your parent or friend to gather several objects around the house. (Don't look at them!) Cover your eyes with a blindfold. Using sound, touch, and smell, try to identify each item. Did you use different senses for each object? Which of your senses was most helpful in figuring out what each object was?

Extra challenge:

You can make this experiment more challenging by gathering objects that are all about the same shape and size. Do you still use the same senses to figure out what everything is?

Taste Test!

It's no secret that holding your nose helps mask the taste of things. That's because 80 percent of what we experience as taste is actually coming from what we're smelling.

You will need . . .

- several different flavored drinks, such as juices, water, and milk
- a cup for each drink

What to do:

Fill each cup with a different flavored drink. Close your eyes and hold your nose. Ask a parent or friend to hand you the drinks one by one. Can you tell what's in the cup? Now keep your eyes closed and taste the drinks in the same order without holding your nose. Did you identify them correctly?

Figure It Out

Our taste buds tell us if what we're eating is salty, sweet, bitter, sour, or savory.

Look at the foods pictured below. Can you figure out which taste category they belong in? If you're not sure, you might want to gather your supplies and start tasting!

SALTY

SWEET

BITTER

SOUR

SAVORY

ANSWER KEY:
grapefruit = bitter, ice cream = sweet
pizza = savory, pickle = sour, popcorn = salty

Keep in Touch!

We experience our sense of touch over our whole body, but some areas have more touch receptors, or sensors, than others and therefore are more sensitive. Test out which areas are the most sensitive!

You will need . . .

- two cotton swabs
- a friend

What to do:

Have your friend close his or her eyes. Holding the cotton swabs close together, gently press them into the back of your friend's hand. Can your friend tell if you are pressing one or two cotton swabs? If your friend feels only one, try holding them a little farther apart. How far apart do the cotton swabs need to be before both are felt? Repeat this experiment on other parts of your body, such as the forehead, shoulder, back, upper arm, inner wrist, back of knee, fingertip, and foot. What areas are the most sensitive? Where is it easiest to feel two cotton swabs? Where do the cotton swabs need to be far apart to tell that there are two?

NATURE AND THE ENVIRONMENT

Did you know that our natural environment is made up of air, water, sunlight, plants, and animals? We need each of these things in order to live, so it's important to learn about nature and the different ways we can help take care of the environment. One of the best ways to do this is to get outside and experience nature firsthand! George is always exploring the world around him. Are you curious about nature and the environment too?

In this section, you'll learn about:

SEA CREATURES AND LIFE UNDERWATER

FOOD CHAINS AND ECOSYSTEMS

THE IMPORTANCE OF PLANTS AND HOW THEY GROW

THE FOUR SEASONS

WEATHER AND CLIMATE

RECYCLING AND TRASH

Curious George DISCOVERS

Ocean

George was a good little monkey and always very curious. Do you want to hear about the time George discovered the ocean? It's hard to believe, but the story starts in the sky.

George had always dreamed of flying, so this was his lucky night.

"Sorry to pick you up so late," Professor Wiseman said. "But a miniature weather satellite just crashed from space. It needs to be found right away, and I think you can help."

Did you know . . .

there are satellites above Earth? They take pictures of how the clouds move. Weather scientists, called meteorologists, use this information to guess when storms will come. You've probably seen satellite photos on weather reports on TV or online.

George and the man with the yellow hat watched from the helicopter as their house got smaller and smaller below. They passed the city, the country, and the beach. Soon they were flying over the ocean. Guess who spotted the ship first?

"Yes, George. There's the Einstein-Pizza research ship just ahead!" the man said.

Professor Einstein and Professor Pizza looked worried.
They explained the situation to George.

"The satellite splashed down close by, but no one is sure
exactly where. It might have broken in the crash!"

That doesn't sound good, does it? What if the information and photographs the satellite had gathered were lost?

"Should we help them look for it?" the man asked.

George couldn't wait to begin.

Did you know . . .
a research ship is a floating laboratory? Some are designed for day trips, but others are home to researchers for weeks or months. Polar research ships can even sail through frozen seas. Can you imagine being captain of a ship that can move through ice? Where would you go if you were?

If they were going to search the ocean floor for the satellite,
they would need to take Pizza and Einstein's submarine.

First a helicopter and now a sub!

Today was turning into a big adventure.

Did you know . . .

sub is short for *submarine*? Subs can travel underwater. Most subs are long and rounded on both ends, which helps them to move easily through the water. Subs can be even smaller than the one George rode in, with room for only one person to travel for a few hours. Some subs are longer than 500 feet and can stay underwater for up to six months. How would you pass the time on a submarine ride that lasted half a year?

Reflected sound waves

Sound waves from ship

What do you think George saw through the sub's windows? There were so many things to look at! Fish, plants . . .

"Okay, George," the man said. "Keep your eyes peeled for that satellite."

George tried to pay attention. Soon the submarine's sonar began to beep. Had they found the satellite already?

"That's not the satellite, George," Professor Wiseman said. "Look!"

The sonar had found a giant sea turtle!

Did you know . . .

giant sea turtles, or leatherback turtles, are the largest of all turtles? They can live for more than fifty years. Leatherbacks are found all over the world. Males never leave the ocean, but a female swims up onto a beach every two to three years to lay eggs in the sand. She'll be gone by the time the baby sea turtles hatch, but they know to head for the water as soon as they climb out of their shells.

It wasn't long before the sonar found the real satellite.

"We're getting close," Professor Wiseman said. "But hold on. We have a problem. The satellite is inside that coral reef!"

Oh no! There was only one way into the reef — through a tiny passage. The sub was much too big to fit. George was so disappointed.

Did you know . . .

coral may look like plants and rocks, but it's actually made up of tiny animals? The animals are called coral polyps. Though reefs are made up of very small animals, they can be huge. The Great Barrier Reef is the largest of all — more than 1,400 miles long!

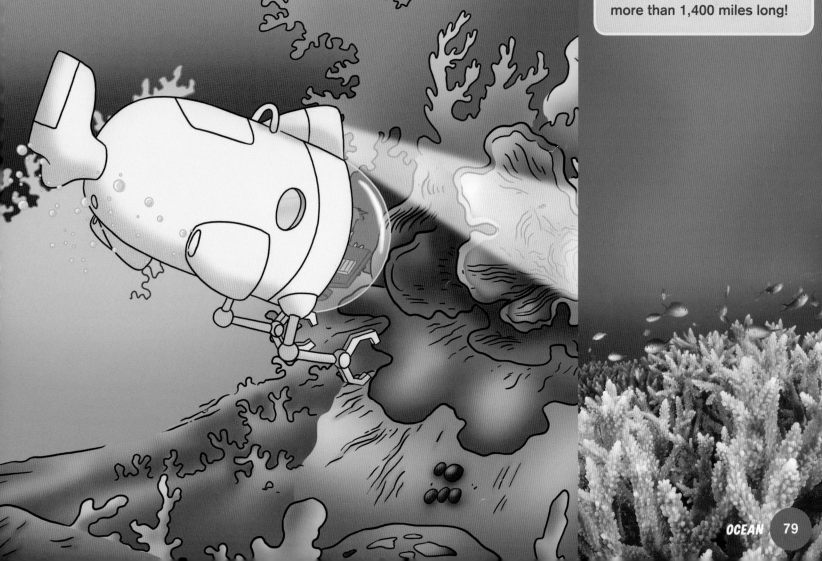

The team returned to the research ship to make a new plan. If the sub was too big to get into the reef, they'd need something smaller. Do you have any ideas?

George had one. *He* was small enough to fit through the opening! With a scuba suit, George could swim in, explore the coral reef, and get the satellite!

George's scuba suit fit just right.

"Your helmet contains a camera, microphone, and headphones. This locator will flash when you're close to the satellite," Professor Wiseman explained. "We'll be able to see you on our monitor and speak to you the whole time. Are you ready?"

George was ready—and excited!

Did you know . . .

scuba stands for self-contained underwater breathing apparatus? George's scuba suit includes an air tank, which will give him the oxygen he needs to breathe underwater. The wetsuit will keep him warm in the cold ocean. If you've ever swum underwater with your eyes open, you know George needs his mask to keep his eyes clear so he can see.

fish and other underwater
animals don't have fins just
for looks? The thin, flat shape
of a fin gives more thrust, or
push, than a small monkey
foot does. As George kicks
with his swim fins, the fins
thrust him through the water
without using much energy.
Their big fins are part of the
reason whales can swim for
hundreds of miles without
getting tired.

The swim fins helped George swim fast!
He swam over and around the coral reef
until he spotted the opening.

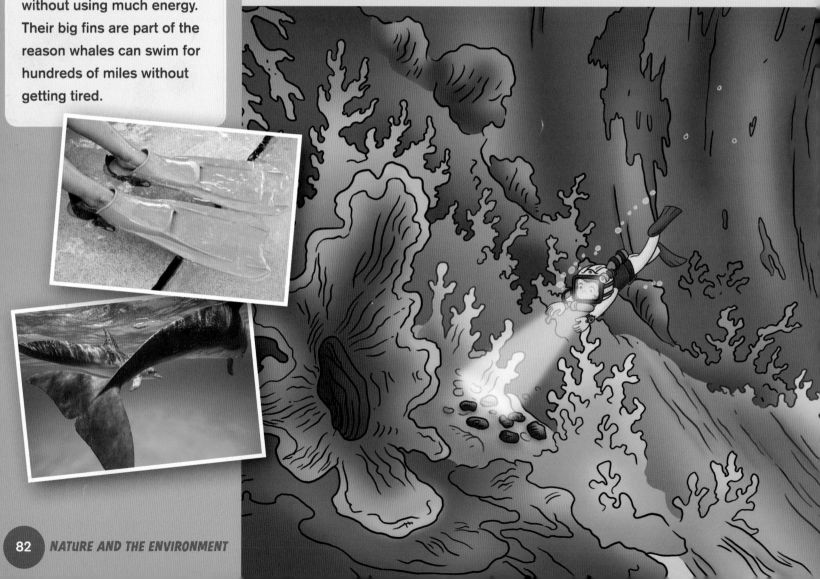

"YOU FOUND THE OPENING, GEORGE!" He could hear Professor Wiseman's voice loud and clear through the speakers in his helmet. *"YOU SHOULD BE ABLE TO SWIM RIGHT THROUGH."*

Once he was inside, George couldn't believe his eyes! Can you believe how many animals live inside the coral reef?

Did you know . . .

coral reefs are home to
some of the most diverse
ecosystems on Earth? That
means many different kinds
of life — plants and animals —
live there all together, relying
on one another for food. An
average reef is home to 3,500
different creatures! Think of
them as the rainforests of
the ocean.

With so many new creatures swimming around him, George never expected to run into someone he recognized! Exploring the coral reef was so much fun that George almost forgot why he was there . . . until he was distracted by a beeping sound. What could it be?

His locator! It was flashing. *"YOU'RE GETTING CLOSE TO THE SATELLITE, GEORGE!"* Professor Wiseman said. George and his new friend swam deeper.

George looked. And looked. The satellite must be here somewhere.

Suddenly, George noticed something strange:
shadows swirled around him on the ocean floor.
Shark-shaped shadows. George was frightened.
He wasn't sure if sharks and monkeys were friends.

Explore further:

Like many ecosystems, the coral reef has a food chain made up of plants, herbivores, and carnivores. Here's how it works:

Reef sharks = carnivores
They eat other animals, such as parrotfish.

Parrotfish = herbivores
They eat plants. such as algae.

Algae = plants
They get their energy from sunlight.

As you may have guessed, monkeys are not part of the coral reef food chain.

"DON'T WORRY, GEORGE. THOSE SMALL REEF SHARKS AREN'T HUNGRY. THE CORAL REEF SUPPLIES THEM WITH ALL THE FOOD THEY NEED," Professor Wiseman explained.

What a relief! George was so distracted by the sharks that it took him a moment to notice what was behind him. It was right there! He had finally found the satellite!

Professor Wiseman flew her helicopter over the reef and lowered a rope down to the sea floor. George grabbed on, and he and the satellite rode out of the water, up to the helicopter, and back to the research ship.

George was happy that he found the satellite. But still, if it was broken, all that work and searching would be for nothing.

When they got back to the ship, Einstein and Pizza checked the satellite.

"It's in great shape!" Professor Pizza said.

"Not a scratch on it!" shouted Professor Einstein.

The research was saved! All thanks to George.

"Ahoy, George!" they called to him from the ship. They wanted to celebrate! But what do you think George was doing?

It had been quite a day. George got to fly in a helicopter, and that was fun. But he decided swimming in the ocean was even better . . . because in the sky there are no sea turtles.

Have you ever wondered where the fruits and vegetables in your grocery store come from? Most of them are grown on farms far away and come by truck, train, boat, or plane. Are you curious about how vegetables and other plants grow? George is curious too.

George was enjoying market day. He liked the fresh vegetable section with its cucumbers, artichokes, beets, spinach, carrots, and onions — to name just a few! George wasn't sure where vegetables came from, but he sure loved to eat them. They had as many different tastes as shapes and colors.

"I was thinking about cooking vegetable soup tonight, George," said his friend the man with the yellow hat.

"But then I started to think of Chef Pisghetti's famous fresh vegetable soup and his spinach ravioli . . . maybe we should go to his restaurant?" the man asked. "What do you think?"

Yum, thought George.

At Chef Pisghetti's restaurant, they sat at their favorite table and placed their order with Netti, the chef's wife.

"We'd both like fresh vegetable soup with extra carrots and spinach ravioli," the man ordered.

"Wait!" Chef Pisghetti cried as he emerged from the kitchen.

"I am out of fresh veggies! We have finished the carrots and spinach."

George was worried. What would they have for dinner?

"Why don't you pick some more vegetables?" Netti asked.

"Would you like to come with me to pick the vegetables, Giorgio?" the chef asked. George nodded and followed him eagerly.

"We're going up to the roof!" the chef announced.

George was confused. Didn't the vegetables come from a market?

"Some veggies grow on farms far away, then travel to a store, where they sit around until you buy them," Chef explained. "But my veggies grow here." The chef proudly waved his arms at all the boxes filled with dirt.

"I pick them, I take them down to my kitchen, and they go into your belly all on the same day! That's Pisghetti fresh." George was still confused. Where were the fresh vegetables?

George watched in amazement as Chef Pisghetti grabbed a sprig of green and pulled a carrot out of the dirt.

Did you know . . .

that plants need sunlight, water, nutrients (food), air, and a safe place to grow? Sounds a lot like what you need to grow too!

"What's this?" Chef Pisghetti pulled another green sprig out of the dirt.
"A weed! Weeds are bad. They soak up the water and nutrients from the
soil that my veggies need to grow," the chef explained. "If I don't have
fresh veggies to cook, I may have to close down!"

George wouldn't want that to happen.

"But I don't have time to pull the weeds out after working all day,"
Chef Pisghetti added.

That night George worried about Chef Pisghetti's weed problem.
He lay in bed while the man read him a bedtime story, but he
didn't pay much attention.

Before he knew it, George had an idea. He knew how he could
help Chef Pisghetti.

The next morning George secretly took some gardening tools from the chef's roof and began to dig up the weeds.

He dug up every green thing he saw. He packed all those leafy greens into three trash bags and threw the bags away.

George was excited to see the chef's reaction in the garden later that day.

But the chef was not happy.

"Oh no!" Chef Pisghetti exclaimed. "The weeds are gone, but all of my veggies are gone too! Who could have done this?" George felt bad. He realized that he didn't know how to tell the difference between a weed and a vegetable. Do you think you could?

Did you know . . .

weeds are plants that grow where they are not wanted? They usually grow quickly and take up space in a garden or on a farm. Weeds use up the nutrients and water that crops need to grow, so they should be removed. Even though weeds can harm crops, some are pretty, such as dandelions.

"I will have to plant all new vegetables," the chef
announced. He took out some seeds to show George.
"Can you believe this little seed will grow into a carrot?"
George shook his head. It was amazing!

The chef dug a small hole in the ground with his trowel, scooping the dirt out. He placed a seed into the hole and replaced the dirt.

"I'll water and fertilize the seeds regularly." The chef saw George's puzzled look. "Fertilize means to feed."

"We will have new vegetables in three to four months," Chef said. "I won't have fresh veggies to use for cooking until then."

George was curious. Why did it take so long? Maybe it didn't have to. Maybe a little monkey could come to the rescue!

George ran home and took all the carrots he could find from the refrigerator.

He ran back to the roof garden and began to dig a hole where the carrot seeds had been planted. George carefully placed one fully grown carrot in each hole that he dug. It took a long time, but finally George finished putting all the carrots he had brought from home in the ground. He put the tools back where he found them.

Test it out!
Sprout a Bean Plant

Take two or three dried lima beans or kidney beans and place them on top of a damp paper towel. Put the paper towel and beans inside a plastic bag and seal it. Put the bag in a warm location with some light, such as a windowsill. Rewet the towel if it dries out. Watch the bean seeds as they begin to sprout. Roots should start to grow after a few days. You can plant the beans in soil at this point and continue to watch the plants grow leaves.

The next morning, Chef Pisghetti found a big surprise!

"My carrots grew this big overnight! It's a miracle," the chef called out.

When George arrived later in the day, Chef Pisghetti was still talking about the carrots.

"Now I won't have to close the restaurant, Giorgio, because I will have fresh veggies."

The chef scratched his head. "I wonder why the eggplants and squash didn't grow."

Oops. George had forgotten all about them.

"Tonight I will plants peas," Chef Pisghetti said. "I hope it works again!"

George left as soon as he could to get more vegetables from his refrigerator. He found fresh eggplants and squash, but no peas. He looked in the cupboards. There were plenty of canned peas. Can you guess what George is going to do?

The next morning the chef found fresh eggplants and squash in his garden, along with canned peas! He called to his wife, "It happened again, Netti. And the peas are in cans! It's magic! Call the TV news!"

The chef was so excited, he asked his scientist friends to come and study the special dirt in his garden.

At home, the man with the yellow hat discovered that all the vegetables in the kitchen were missing. "George," he called, "do you know what happened to all our veggies?"

George nodded. He led his friend out of the house and over to Chef Pisghetti's.

When the man arrived at the rooftop garden, he finally understood what George had done. "Well, it looks like George has been your magic gardener," the man explained. "All our vegetables have been going into your dirt."

"Ah, Netti, our garden isn't magic after all," the chef said sadly.

"But your cooking still is," Netti replied.

"Absolutely!" everyone agreed.

"That's right," said the man, "you can cook up our vegetables any day!"

Everyone helped pick the vegetables, and Chef Pisghetti invited all his friends to stay for a delicious lunch of vegetable soup. George's plan was a success after all!

George was a good little monkey and always very curious.
Do you want to hear about the time George's curiosity helped
him learn all about the seasons?

It all started on a cold winter day. The leaves were gone and the grass was brown, but there wasn't a snowflake in sight. George had to bundle up in his winter coat. But when he got outside, he wasn't sure what to do.

There were no fallen leaves to play in. There were no birds to watch. George had toys for warm days and toys for snowy days, but nothing for just plain cold days.

George had an idea. He would visit with the bunnies! But when he went next door, the bunnies weren't in their hutch. He found his friend Bill and the bunnies inside.

"I'm going to bring them to my grandmother's house for the winter, George," Bill told him. "It's just too cold here to keep the bunnies outside in their house."

George was disappointed to see the bunnies go. Then Bill asked him to do a special job. "While I'm away, will you feed Jumpy Squirrel for me?" he asked. "There aren't a lot of nuts and seeds around in winter, so it's an important job." George was happy to help!

George fed Jumpy, but that took only a minute.

He wasn't sure what to do after that.

He looked around his yard and thought about summer. He missed his pool and blowing bubbles.

Everything fun seemed to happen in the spring, summer, or fall. Winter was the most boring season.

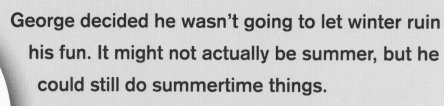

George decided he wasn't going to let winter ruin his fun. It might not actually be summer, but he could still do summertime things.

George got the hose and filled his little pool with water. But when he jumped in, the water was so cold! George got cold too. Brrr . . .

Did you know . . .

large bodies of water take longer to heat up—and cool down—than air does? This is why even though the air temperature in the summer can get very hot, the water in a big lake or the ocean is still nice and cool!

He ran into the house. "Soak your feet in warm water to get rid of the chill," the man with the yellow hat said. The warm bath was a lot nicer than the cold pool. George felt much better.

The next day it was even colder! George bundled into his coat and scarf when he went out to play. He wanted to enjoy being outside in the winter as much as he would in the other seasons. He sat by his pool to relax.

Then George blew some bubbles for Jumpy. But when Jumpy
tried to pop a bubble, they discovered that it had frozen.
George didn't know bubbles could freeze.

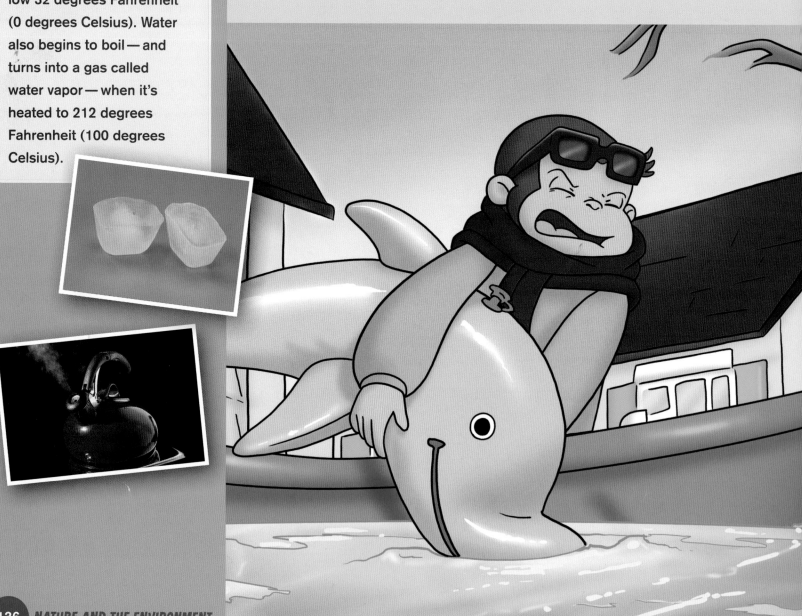

Did you know . . .

water can take the form of a solid, a liquid, or a gas? Liquid water starts to freeze and become solid ice when the temperature drops below 32 degrees Fahrenheit (0 degrees Celsius). Water also begins to boil — and turns into a gas called water vapor — when it's heated to 212 degrees Fahrenheit (100 degrees Celsius).

That was a surprise! Then George noticed something even more surprising: the water in the pool had frozen. Yesterday's summer fun had turned into today's giant ice cube!

George was starting to feel like an ice cube too. He went inside to warm up and drink some hot cocoa.

George was puzzled. How could a monkey have any fun outside when everything kept freezing?

Suddenly, George had an idea! He could use frozen things to make a game. He filled a balloon and several cartons from the recycling bin with water.

Then he brought them outside so they would freeze in the cold air.

George didn't notice when Jumpy accidentally spilled some seeds and nuts into the cartons of water.

The next morning was the coldest day yet! George had to wear a hat, scarf, and coat to stay warm. He didn't mind, though. He went to check on the balloon and cartons of water he'd left out the night before. They were frozen solid! George couldn't wait to set them up for a game of icy winter bowling.

When he took the ice from the cartons, though, he realized that some of Jumpy's nuts and seeds were frozen inside. Oh well. George decided to try to bowl anyway.

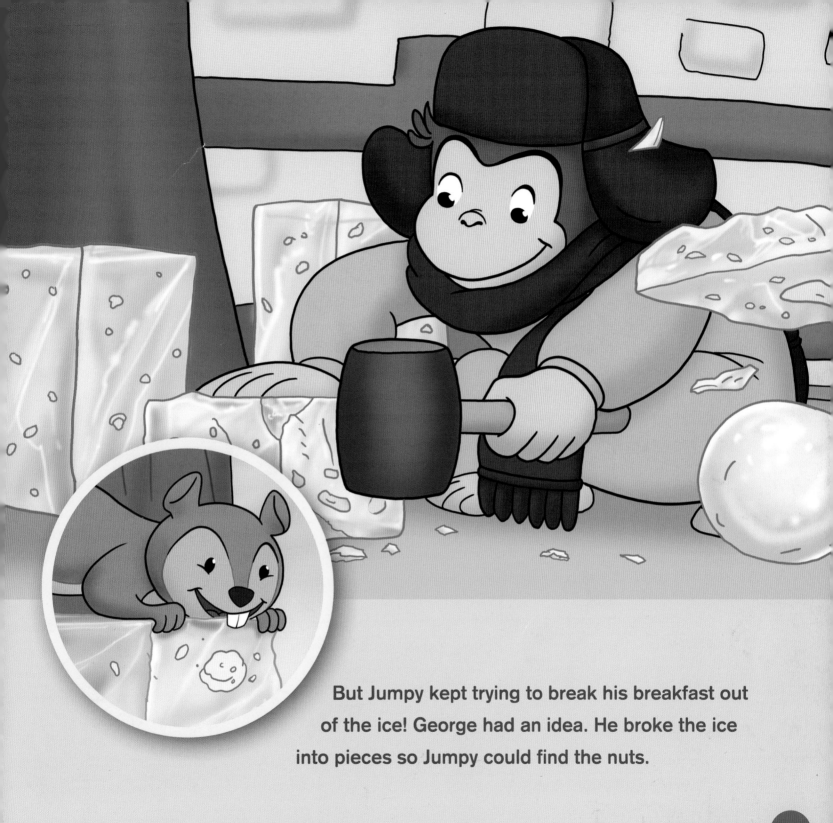

But Jumpy kept trying to break his breakfast out of the ice! George had an idea. He broke the ice into pieces so Jumpy could find the nuts.

The pieces slid on the ground and Jumpy chased after them. George and Jumpy knocked the ice blocks around until the sun went down. It wasn't ice bowling, but it was just as fun!

Besides, George knew he could try his new bowling invention again the next day. He filled the cartons and balloon with water once more and left them outside.

In the morning, George bundled up. "You're not going to need that hat and scarf today, George," his friend said. George went outside. It felt more like spring or fall than winter.

George checked on his cartons and balloon, hoping for another round of ice bowling. But the water hadn't turned to ice — it was too warm for it to freeze!

Did you know . . .

even if you live in a place with a cold winter climate, you can still have warm winter days? That's because climate and weather are two different things. Climate means what you can expect a whole season to feel like on average—the summer is warm, the winter is cold. But weather is all about the day-to-day changes in wind, sunlight, clouds, and storms. So, like George, you could have a warm, sunny day in winter and a chilly, gray day in summer.

The weather was very confusing. Wasn't it supposed to be cold in the winter and warmer in the other seasons? George went back into the house.

But later that day, something amazing happened! George thought he saw something outside his window. When he went to look, it was snowing.

George thought that if it was cold enough to snow, it might be cold enough for water to freeze again. And cold enough to make a new ice bowling set. Maybe the cold could be fun after all!

George realized that winter, spring, summer, and fall were all great in their own way. But the pool could wait until summer.

Right now, he had winter toys to play with—
and a whole chilly season to enjoy!

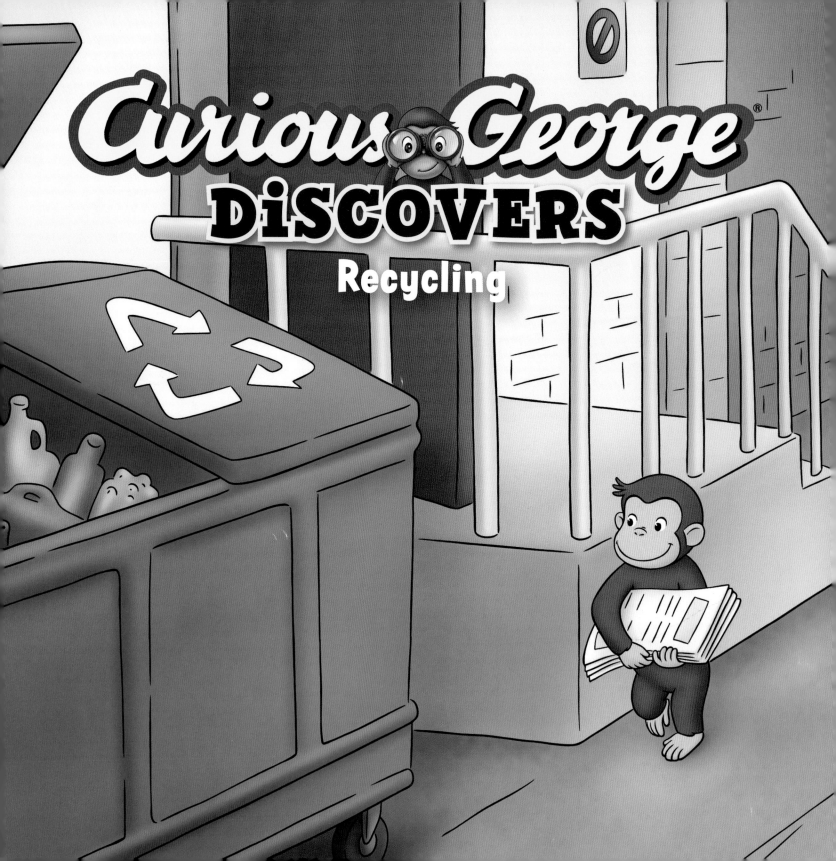

George was a good little monkey, and always very curious. He was especially curious about protecting our environment and keeping the planet clean. Do you want to learn all about recycling with George?

George had been getting ready to throw away a big bag of trash.

As he was about to lift the heavy load into the garbage chute, he
heard the doorman shout, "Wait! Are you sure that trash is all trash?"

George didn't know what the doorman could be talking about.
The bag was filled with things that George and his friend the man
with the yellow hat no longer needed and were ready to throw away.

"We need to separate recyclables from trash," the doorman told George, taking the bag. He grabbed a few of the items and tossed them in some big blue bins labeled with arrows. "Recycling makes our planet a lot neater, George! And on top of that," he said, handing him a flyer, "there's a contest for the city's apartment buildings. The building that collects the most recycling wins!"

That all sounded great to George . . . except he didn't know what recycling *was*.

George wanted to help recycle, once he figured out how to do it. George showed the flyer to the man.

"Recycling makes old bottles and cans into *new* bottles and cans. Otherwise trash would just pile up all over the planet," said the man with the yellow hat.

This made George very worried. He didn't like thinking about Earth covered in trash.

The man with the yellow hat could tell George was concerned. He had an idea.

"Say, George, would you like to visit the recycling center? Then you can see how this whole thing works." Just a few minutes ago, George didn't even know what recycling was. Now he was going to see it in action!

On their way out, they saw the doorman bringing recyclables to the outside bins for the contest. "We're off to an impressive start!" the doorman said.

George and his friend arrived at the recycling center. George saw four big pictures hanging above four big containers. There was a cardboard box, a glass bottle, a tin can, and a plastic jug.

Being a curious monkey, George jumped right into the bin full of glass bottles and jars. Just then a man who worked at the recycling center came over. "My monkey would like to see what recycling is all about," said the man with the yellow hat.

The worker took a glass jar from George's hands, turned it over, and pointed to the bottom. There was something George had never noticed before: three arrows shaped like a triangle.

"When you see three arrows like this, it means the item can be recycled," the worker said. "Come with me."

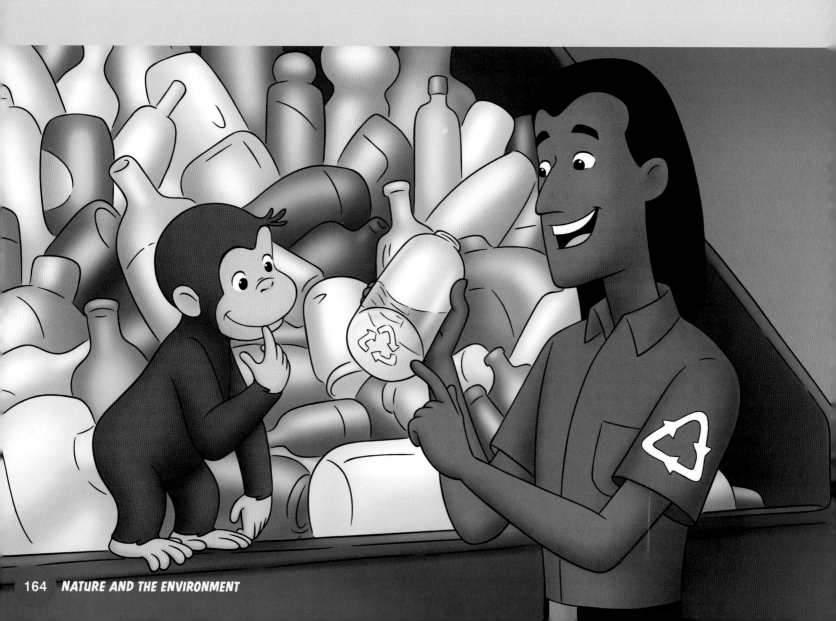

Test it out!

When you see arrows with a number in the middle, the number indicates what the material is made of. Go into your kitchen cabinets and refrigerator and take a look at the containers you might find. Do you see any arrows? What do they say? How many things did you find with arrows on them? Do you and your family recycle these items?

"Once the item gets to the recycling center, the next step is for it to be sorted properly, and then cleaned," the worker explained. George saw lots of jars, bottles, and containers cruising down a conveyor belt. They were going to end up in those big bins he'd seen.

Explore further:

Plastic and glass containers are sent to a recycling center. There they are broken down into smaller bits, melted, and then made into even smaller pieces called granules. Lots of things are made from granules, like more plastic and glass bottles, window frames, and even outdoor furniture.

The worker then showed George a poster. It explained the recycling process. "Recycled glass is broken into small bits, and then melted down. Plastic, too," he said.

Even recycled paper could be broken down to make new paper. George could hardly believe this was all possible. There was so much to recycle!

Test it out!
Paper vs. Plastic

Plastic can take hundreds of years to completely de-compose, or break down, in nature. Paper will decompose more quickly, especially in wet conditions. Try wetting a plastic bag and wetting a paper bag. This can show you how both react to an element such as water. You can even try leaving one of each in your backyard for a day, a week, or even a month. Check on each bag to see what's happened to it as it's been exposed to sun, rain, heat, and more. What are your observations?

Back at the apartment, the competition was heating up and the doorman was worried they were falling behind. Thanks to his visit to the recycling center, George had some good ideas about how he could help recycle. He went upstairs to get started.

In the refrigerator George saw lots of containers he could turn in for the recycling contest. But none of them were empty. The olive jar only had a *few* olives left in it. And the ketchup container was only half full . . . what if George just combined them?

When George finished going through the refrigerator, he moved on to the rest of the apartment building.

He saw big plastic paint buckets with the arrows on the bottom! He took them.

He saw a grocery delivery just sitting outside an apartment door. He took the shampoo and juice bottles.

A stack of pizza coupons? That paper could be recycled! He took the whole pile.

All of these things would help fill his building's recycling bins. George was so happy to be helping and recycling.

While George was collecting these items, the doorman was talking to the door-woman next door. Her building was competing in the recycling contest as well. "The more people recycle, the better it is for the Earth," she said. "And if your building participates in some reuse programs, you'll help the planet even more!"

The doorman didn't know the difference between reusing and recycling. The doorwoman explained that reusing simply means using something again. In her building, people leave their magazines in a common area for other people to read. Instead of throwing away moving boxes, they kept them in the basement for other people to use when they needed them.

Did you know . . .
there are lots of ways to help the environment? Have you heard about reduce, reuse, recycle? Reduce means to cut down on the amount of stuff you use every day. For example, instead of using disposable plastic water bottles, you can put your water in a glass or metal bottle to reduce the amount of plastic you use. Reuse means to take the things you've already used and find a way to use them again. Handing down your clothes to friends or younger siblings is a good way to reuse perfectly good pants and shirts. And, of course, you already know lots about recycling by now!

"Hey, I reuse my shopping bags!" said the doorman.
He was already doing it.

When the doorman returned to his recycling bins, they were all filled to the top! The doorwoman was impressed. But the doorman wasn't sure where all this stuff had come from, until . . .

"Someone took my paint pails!"

"My groceries were stolen!"

"Where are our pizza coupons?"

All of their items were in the recycling bins! The doorman was confused. But just then, George came outside carrying another stack of newspapers.

The man with the yellow hat was right behind him. "I think *I* know where the extra recycling came from," the man said, holding his olive jar, which was full of ketchup. "George, you recycle things *after* you use them."

Oops! George had forgotten that part.

After George and the doorman returned all of the extra items, it turned out to be a tie with the doorwoman's building! The two buildings could share the trophy.

George eyed the three big arrows on the front of the trophy.

"That's not recycling, George!" They all laughed.

George would get the hang of recycling soon enough!

THERE'S MORE TO EXPLORE ABOUT THE WORLD AROUND US!

Reflected sound waves

Sound waves from ship

Exploring Sonar

George and his friends used sonar to find the satellite on the ocean floor. Listening to sound waves bouncing off objects underwater helps oceanographers figure out how far they are from what they're looking for — coral reefs, trenches, or lost satellites! You can guess where you are in a room with your eyes closed the same way.

Test it out!

You will need . . .

- an empty room, like your garage or the school gym

- your ears

- your loudest voice

Stand in the empty room, close your eyes, tune up your ears, and make some noise! How does the echo sound when you stand in the middle of the room? How about when you stand in the corner or close to a wall? How does the echo change based on your position?

Echoes sound longer when you are farther away from a wall because it takes longer for the sound waves to reach the wall and bounce back to your ears. Sonar works the same way. Oceanographers use it to map the ocean floor. If the sound waves bounce back quickly, the floor is close. If they take longer, the floor is farther away and the water is deeper.

Who's Hungry?

Can you sort the organisms into these categories:
carnivores, herbivores, and **plants?**

ALGAE	GRAIN	MOUSE
CLOVER	GRASS	RABBIT
PARROTFISH	HOUSECAT	SHARK
ZEBRA	LION	WOLF

Now can you use the animals to make a food chain for each of these ecosystems?

CORAL REEF
SAVANNAH
FOREST
BACKYARD

Here's an example:

shark < parrotfish < algae = coral reef.
In the coral reef, sharks hunt parrotfish and parrotfish eat algae.

ANSWER KEY:

plants — algae, clover, grain, grass
herbivores — parrotfish, rabbit, zebra, mouse
carnivores — shark, wolf, lion, housecat

ANSWER KEY:

coral reef — shark < parrotfish < algae
savannah — lion < zebra < grass
forest — wolf < rabbit < clover
backyard — housecat < mouse < grain

Drink Up!

You already learned that a plant needs sunlight, air, water, and a good place to grow. Plants use these things to make their own food. They get most of the water they need by soaking it up from the soil through their roots and stems. Try this exciting experiment to see how plants absorb water and nutrients.

You will need . . .

- 4 glasses
- water
- red, yellow, blue, and green food coloring
- 4 Napa cabbage leaves or white flowers (such as carnations or daisies)

What to do:

1. Fill your glasses halfway up with water.
2. Pour a generous amount of a different colored food dye into each glass (make sure the water is very brightly colored!).
3. Add a single cabbage leaf or flower to each glass.
4. Let your plants sit overnight so that they have plenty of time to absorb some of the colorful water. You may want to take before and after photos. Check out the amazing results the next day! You can see how the water was absorbed by the plant by the way the food coloring has spread through it. Isn't science lovely?

Veggies All Year Round

How many different vegetables are there? Too many to list! But there are some veggies that you can easily find each season. Look at the lists below and count how many you've tried. Which are your favorites? Can you try one new vegetable every week? You can find lots of yummy recipes online.

Winter	Spring	Summer	Fall
Beets	Artichokes	Bell Peppers	Cabbage
Brussels Sprouts	Asparagus	Cucumbers	Cauliflower
Leeks	Broccoli	Eggplant	Collard Greens
Onions	Carrots	Green Beans	Ginger
Parsnips	Celery	Lima Beans	Kale
Lettuce	Garlic	Mushrooms	Peas
Mushrooms	Corn	Onions	Potatoes
Pumpkins	Rhubarb	Okra	Radishes
Rutabagas	Swiss Chard	Summer Squash & Zucchini	Spinach
Winter Squash	Turnips	Tomatoes	Sweet Potatoes & Yams

Exploring the Seasons: Winter, Spring, Summer, Fall

George had a case of the winter blues, but then he discovered that no matter what the season, there are lots of great things to do. While you can only jump in colorful leaves in the fall and watch new things sprout and grow in spring, you can watch the weather any time of year and keep track of what you learn about each season's traits by starting your very own weather journal.

You will need . . .

- a notebook
- markers, crayons, or colored pencils
- your five senses

What to do:

First, write down the date so you know which day and season it is when you look back through your journal. Then write down a few words about what the weather looks like that day. Is it sunny, rainy, cloudy, windy? Does the temperature feel cold or warm — or dry or humid? What can you smell when you take a deep breath?

Once you write down your description, it's time to illustrate! Use your crayons, markers, or colored pencils to draw a picture of what the day looks like, being sure to capture as many details and colors of the season as you can. You can write in your weather journal every day, or even once a week or once a month, to help keep track of how the seasons change near you!

Who's Hungry? You Are!

Here's a frosty—and healthy—treat you can make and enjoy whenever you need a snack.

You will need . . .

- your favorite fruit juice
- ice pop molds (or an ice cube tray with waxed paper and toothpicks or craft sticks)

What to do:

Ask a parent or friend to help you fill an ice pop mold. If you don't have one, fill the segments of the ice cube tray with juice and then cover with waxed paper. Stick one toothpick or craft stick through the waxed paper into each segment of juice. This will help keep the sticks in place as the juice freezes. Put the mold or ice cube tray in the freezer for about four hours until frozen solid. Enjoy a frosty treat.

Explore Further

Do different liquids freeze at different temperatures? You can find out—and track your results!

You will need . . .

- small paper cups
- water and other liquids (juice, oil, milk, soda)
- a cookie sheet
- a clock or timer
- paper and pen

What to do:

Place the paper cups on the cookie sheet, then fill each cup halfway with a different liquid. Carefully place the sheet in the freezer. Set your timer for a half hour. While you wait, make a chart of the liquids you used and leave a space to fill in how long it takes for each to freeze. Check on the cups when the timer goes off. Is anything frozen yet? Check again in another half hour and another. Keep track of how long it takes for each type of liquid to freeze!

RECYCLED CRAFTS

There are lots of things you can make at home with some of the materials you are probably already recycling: plastic bottles and cardboard.

RECYCLED BOTTLE BIRD FEEDER

You will need . . .

- a clean, empty half-gallon milk container or two-liter soda bottle
- birdseed
- a piece of twine or sturdy string

What to do:

1. Get a grownup to help you cut a hole in the side of your plastic bottle. Make the hole about halfway up the side of the bottle.
2. Fill the bottle with birdseed and then tie a piece of twine around the bottle's lid. You can make this as long or as short as you'd like so that you can hang it from a branch or railing.
3. Then wait for the birds to come check out your feeder! Birds especially love having extra seeds to eat in the wintertime.

RECYCLED ROBOT!

You will need . . .

- an empty cereal box
- a smaller box, such as an empty macaroni and cheese box
- 4 empty toilet paper or paper towel rolls
- glue
- tinfoil scraps
- craft supplies, such as glitter, pompoms, bottle caps, sequins, buttons, and feathers

What to do:

1. Have a grownup help you cut one circle on each side of a cereal box and two in the bottom. This is where you can insert your robot's toilet paper–roll arms and legs.
2. Once your robot has arms and legs, glue your smaller box on top of the cereal box—this will be your robot's head!
3. Glue tinfoil over all the cardboard to make your robot look like he's made of metal.
4. Now you are all set to decorate! You can use craft supplies or anything you can find from your recycling to make your robot as shiny and unique as you can imagine.

REDUCE, REUSE, RECYCLE

Did you know . . .

that nearly 100 percent of a computer can be recycled? Computers are made up of a lot of recyclable material, including plastic, metal, and glass. You may be surprised to know that there are lots of things beyond water bottles and newspapers that can be recycled. Some places recycle batteries, light bulbs, used CDs and DVDs—and yes, even electronics like computers and cell phones. Ask a grownup to help you look online to see what other kinds of things you and your family could be recycling.

How much trash do you throw away? Keep track of everything you throw away for a day: papers, plastics, magazines, cans, even food. You might be surprised!

Once you have your list of all the things you threw out, try to come up with some ways to reduce, reuse, or recycle more of the things you put in the trash each day.

TRASH OR RECYCLING?

Can you figure out what items below are meant to be recycled or reused, and which should be thrown away?

ANSWER KEY:
Recyclables: can, jar, newspaper, cereal box, juice container, paper bag
Trash: banana peel, pizza, candy wrapper, napkin, Styrofoam cup

THE SKY AND SPACE

Have you ever looked up at the sky and wondered what else is out there? The planet Earth is part of a great big universe, along with the sun, moon, stars, and all the other planets. In fact, the universe is made up of everything we can sense, measure, or observe. Scientists are learning more about our universe every day, but there's still so much to discover! Are you curious about the sky and space? George is too!

In this section, you'll learn about:

OUR SOLAR SYSTEM

GRAVITY AND ORBITS

THE DAY SKY AND THE NIGHT SKY

THE STARS AND CONSTELLATIONS

Have you ever wondered how many stars there are in the sky? George has — especially when he's in the country. In the country, the summer nights are cool, you can hear frogs croaking, and the sky is full of stars.

Did you know . . .

scientists who study stars are called astronomers? People have looked at the stars and wondered about the mysteries of space for thousands of years. Early astronomers used the stars in the sky to find their way and to make calendars. We still use some of their methods today.

One night, George was outside looking at the sky when he heard Bill's voice.

"Hi, George! It's a great night for stargazing," Bill called from his window. But George wasn't just looking at the stars. He was trying to figure out how many stars there were in the sky—there must be hundreds! "Not even scientists know how many stars are up there," Bill said.

George thought it was time somebody found out!

George knew the most important rule of counting anything was
keeping track. He found a notepad and pencil and made a mark for
each star as he counted it. There were so many stars to keep track
of, but he kept at it: one, two, three, four, five . . .

But George fell asleep midcount! That was okay. After a good night's rest he would be ready to start counting again the next night.

There was only one problem: his counting system didn't keep track of which stars he had already counted. So last night's count didn't count! George figured the only way he could count the stars without losing track was to count all the stars really fast before he fell asleep.

But George wasn't fast enough.

Bill stopped by the following day. "Morning, fellas!"

The man waved, but George still felt sleepy. "George
was up late counting stars," the man said.

"Too bad you can't count stars during the day. They are always up there, you know," Bill said. "We just can't see them because the sun is so bright."

that Bill was right? The sun, moon, and stars are always in the sky, but we can see them only at certain times. Our eyes can't see the small lights of the stars during the day because of the big light of the sun.

Test it out!

Try this experiment: Sit in a dark room and turn on a flashlight. Notice how bright the flashlight is in the dark. Now turn on the lights in the room and keep your flashlight on. Does the flashlight still look as bright as it did when the room was dark?

George wasn't so sure. He wondered what really happened to stars during the day. Maybe they went to sleep, or got blown out like candles on a birthday cake. Wherever they went, George couldn't count stars he couldn't see.

"There are lots of differences between the sky during the day and the sky at night," the man said. "We can see the moon and the stars at night, but we can see the sun only during the day."

"Right!" said Bill. "Because at night, the sun is shining on the other side of Earth. When it's nighttime here, it's daytime there!"

When it came to day sky and night sky, George was sure about two things: he couldn't count stars during the day, and he couldn't count all of the stars in one night. But he wasn't going to give up.

Did you know . . .
that the sun and the moon are very different? The sun is a star that gives off the heat and energy that plants and animals on Earth need to live. The sun stays in the same spot while Earth spins and moves in a circle around the sun. This is called orbiting. The moon is made up mostly of rock. Though it looks bright, it can't make light. It reflects light from the sun. The moon orbits the Earth.

George took a good long look at the night sky. The stars were scattered around like confetti. And, like confetti, there wasn't a pattern to the way they were arranged. Unless . . .

George noticed a group of stars that looked familiar. They looked like a big upside-down cap!

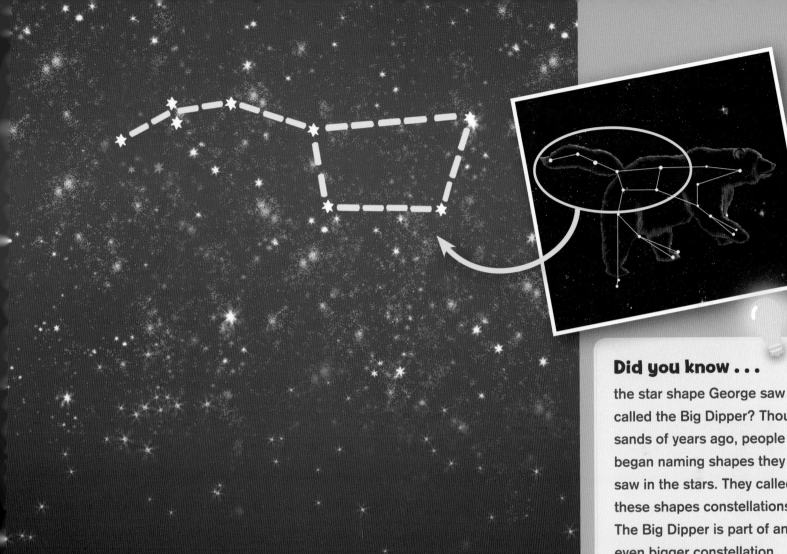

Did you know . . .

the star shape George saw is called the Big Dipper? Thousands of years ago, people began naming shapes they saw in the stars. They called these shapes constellations. The Big Dipper is part of an even bigger constellation called the Great Bear. There are eighty-eight constellations in all. Many of them still have their ancient names, such as Orion, Leo, and Scorpio. These star shapes were named by astronomers and used to map the sky, just like George did.

George could use this star shape as a place-keeper. He counted the stars below it and marked them on his pad. Then he counted the stars above it and on each side.

George had a system! He could use star shapes to keep track of
which stars he had already counted. When he got tired, he could go
to bed and know where he left off for the next night's count.

At the end of the week, it was time for George and the man to return to the city. George had made a lot of progress on his star-counting. And now that he had a system, he could count stars in the city, too. "Big, hot city, here we come!" the man said.

Did you know . . .

that the night sky looks different depending on where you are on Earth? You can see different constellations from North America than you can from Australia, on the other side of the planet. Lucky for George, the big city is close enough to the country house that the sky is the same in both places.

The city was very hot. George couldn't wait to
get into the cool, air-conditioned lobby.

But it was just as warm inside their building as it was outside.

"Is the air conditioner broken?" the man asked.

"No," said the doorman. "But we're not allowed to use it.
You'll have to keep yours off in your apartment, too."

George wondered why. "Too many air conditioners running at once uses a lot of electricity. It can cause the power to go out," the man said. "I guess we'll be a little warm tonight."

But George wasn't worried about electricity and being too hot. He had stars to count!

George knew he would have a great view of the sky from the roof. But when he got up there and looked around, he noticed something strange. In the city, he couldn't see any stars at all!

George can't see the stars because there is too much man-made light in the city? Just like the sun outshining the stars during the day, the streetlights and lights from city buildings are bright enough to block out the natural light of the stars at night.

George went back to the apartment to see his friend. "It's tough to count stars in the big, bright city," the man explained. George was confused. "It's like trying to count stars during the daytime. They're up there, but we can't see them."

With no stars to count, George figured he might as well go to bed. But it was too hot to sleep. The one time he could have stayed awake all night long to count, he couldn't see a single star!

George took a walk out onto the balcony. His neighbors had their air conditioners on. George could hear them humming. Would it really hurt if he turned their AC on? Just for a minute?

The cold air felt good on George's face. But a moment later,
the AC — and all of the lights in the apartment — went out!

Did you know . . .

that "blackout" is another word for a power outage? A blackout can happen for a lot of reasons. Windy weather and falling trees can damage power lines, for example. And if too many people in one area use a lot of electricity at the same time, the system might shut down. Important buildings like hospitals have backup generators that can give them power during a blackout.

George ran back up to the roof. Uh-oh. The lights were out in all the buildings around them. Could one curious little monkey cause a citywide blackout? George didn't know, but there was only one thing to do at a time like this — hide!

Before long the man found George in his hiding spot.
George was upset about turning off the city's electricity.
"It wasn't your fault, George!" the man said. "It takes
more than one little monkey to cause a blackout."

Just then the doorman and Hundley joined them on the roof.
"This blackout's really something, isn't it?" the doorman asked.

"Yes," said the man. "But George thinks the blackout was his
fault. He turned on our air conditioner."

"I thought it was my fault, too!" said the doorman. "Hundley
was so hot, I turned on our AC for just a minute. Then all the
lights went out. I bet a lot people thought the same thing."
George was relieved!

"Well, George, there is one good thing about this blackout. Now you can see the stars!" It was true! Now that all of the electrical lights were out and the city was dark, he could see the sky full of stars again. George found the Big Upside-Down Cap and settled in for a good, long star-count.

Curious George® DISCOVERS

Space

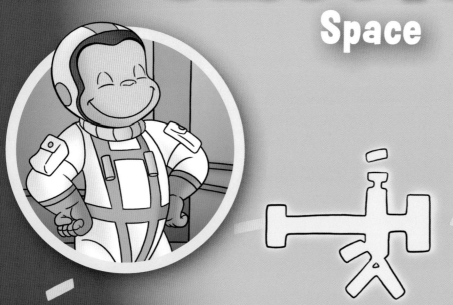

Are you curious about outer space?
George is too! Come along and see
what's happening at the space center . . .

Professor Wiseman invited George and his friend the man with the yellow hat to visit her at the space center. Professor Einstein and Professor Pizza needed help, and she thought they might be able to lend a hand. Or more than one, as it turned out.

"How can we help?" asked the man.

The scientists began to brief the man on his first mission: to restock the space station's food supply. The astronauts on the station had discovered they had only one peanut left to eat.

The man with the yellow hat was planning to ride a space shuttle up through Earth's atmosphere into space. He would enter orbit around Earth and pass near the space station in order to make his delivery. The man would get to experience weightlessness!

How would you like to float inside a spaceship? Of course, George was disappointed he wouldn't be able to come along.

Did you know . . .

that gravity is the force pulling all objects on the surface of a planet toward the center of that planet? It keeps us from floating off into space! Gravity is weaker the farther you are from the center of a planet. If you are far enough away, you are weightless and float.

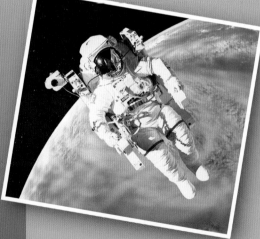

But in order for the man to release the supplies, he needed to be able to push four buttons at the same time. The man only had two hands. He couldn't do that, but a monkey could. George was thrilled to help!

The hungry scientists on the space station would soon have more than one peanut to eat. George would also deliver some new supplies to help them with science experiments.

"You must launch the payload at exactly the right moment," Professor Einstein said to George. George nodded. He would have to listen to instructions carefully. Do you think that would be hard for one little monkey?

Did you know . . .

that *payload* is another word for cargo? That means the materials that a vehicle is carrying.

Liftoff was a success, but then George wanted to look at the supplies. He took them out to play, but he couldn't get them back inside quickly enough. George missed the payload launch! He passed right by the space station without sending the supplies.

George would have to orbit Earth
one more time!

Did you know . . .

to orbit the Earth means
to follow a path in space
around our planet?
When the spaceship
travels, it's like a
tug-of-war between
the force pulling the
ship back down to
Earth and the speed
of the ship going
forward. When the
speed is just right, the
ship can travel in a circle
around the Earth forever.

"George, you have enough fuel for only one more orbit. You have to get the supplies back in their containers. The next time you pass the station will be the last chance. Then we have to bring you home," warned Professor Wiseman.

George was used to cleaning his room. It was good practice for cleaning up the mess in the spaceship.

He was ready in time to launch the supplies.

Hooray! They made it to the space station!

Did you know . . .

that George isn't the first monkey in space? Many different kinds of animals have been launched into space and returned safely to Earth: monkeys, dogs, cats, turtles, butterflies, fish, rabbits, mice, spiders, and more. Studying animals in space helps scientists learn about living in a weightless environment.

George had one more task to complete. He had to make it back to the ground safely! To do this the shuttle had to reenter Earth's atmosphere at the right moment.

Did you know . . .

that to land, the shuttle must make a change in direction, which slows the ship down so it falls back to Earth? The ship is coated with a material that can handle the heat created as the ship passes through the atmosphere at such a great speed. The shuttle has a special shape that helps keep it cool and slow it down. It also uses a parachute to slow down safely once it has touched down on the ground.

Did you know . . .

NASA ended the space shuttle program in 2011? Now U.S. astronauts travel to the International Space Station aboard the Russian spacecraft *Soyuz* at a price of $70 million per ride. That's one expensive ticket!

It was a good thing George listened to instructions this time. He pulled the lever that controlled the ship's direction. He could now land the ship back at the space center. His friends congratulated him on a successful mission!

"On to our next problem . . ." said Professor Pizza, once the shuttle mission was over. "We are having trouble with our Mars rover."

"The controls are getting stuck here at the space center. We are worried that when it actually lands on Mars it will also get stuck on the rocks," added Professor Einstein.

"A Mars rover is a vehicle specially made for exploring the Red Planet and sending information back to Earth," the man explained. "They're testing the new rover here at the space center."

Did you know . . .

Mars is the fourth planet in our solar system? It is smaller and lighter than Earth. Iron oxide, or rust, gives the soil a reddish color, which is why Mars is also known as the Red Planet. Scientists are interested in knowing all about our next-door neighbor in the hope that someday people will be able to visit Mars. Would you like to visit Mars?

George thought the Mars rovers would be fun to drive. But he soon learned that they are operated by remote control only.

Professor Einstein offered everyone a piece of chewing gum as he explained the sticky situation in the space control center. "You know there's a no-gum rule in here, Einstein," said Professor Pizza. "Ah, you're right," said Professor Einstein. He opened a large metal drawer and threw his gum out.

George was excited to see the launch of the latest Mars rover. He hoped they could figure out this problem together. They sat around a table to talk and plan.

The man asked, "Since Mars has lower gravity than Earth, is it possible the problem wouldn't even happen there?"

Professor Pizza agreed. "That's certainly possible. If the pull of Earth's gravity is causing the sticking, it might not stick in Mars's low gravity."

"With the lower gravity on Mars, you would be three times stronger there," said Professor Wiseman. "If the rover sticks, maybe we can get it going again by giving it a good push."

George imagined how strong he would be on Mars.

Did you know . . .

that the gravity on Mars is 38 percent of the gravity on Earth? That means that if you weighed 100 pounds on Earth, you would weigh 38 pounds on Mars.

Earth 49.2
Mars 18.696

Test it out!

Using a bathroom scale, weigh yourself. Write the number down. Now ask an adult to help you multiply that number by 0.38 to get the amount you would weigh on Mars.

George wanted to help, but he was tired and nothing puts a monkey to sleep like a lot of adults talking. The last thing George heard the man saying was "If only we could send someone to Mars to push it . . ."

George fell fast asleep. He dreamed he was going to be the first monkey headed to Mars!

Did you know . . .

there have been four Mars rovers sent to explore the surface of Mars? NASA scientists develop and test the rovers here first. Then they send the vehicles by themselves to explore the surface of the Red Planet. The rovers do experiments on rock samples and send the information back to Earth. The Mars rovers helped scientists learn that there is water in the form of ice on Mars. We hope the rovers will also tell us if life exists there now or did in the past.

In his dream, Professor Wiseman told him, "It's an important mission, George. If the rover sticks, your job is to give it a good push."

The man was going on the space mission with George—how lucky! George wouldn't be lonely on his trip.

When the ship finally landed on Mars, George was sitting on top of the Mars rover. When it was released, he went with it! The rover bounced along the surface of the Red Planet. George was on a runaway vehicle!

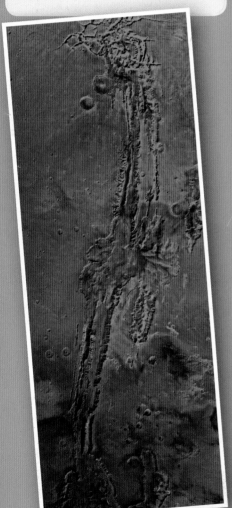

Lucky for George, he found the remote that controlled the rover. He was able to slow down the rover. Whew. He also had a book about the Mars terrain. Now he could explore Mars!

George rolled up to a very deep, very wide valley that looked like the Grand Canyon, only much larger. The book told him it was called the Valles Marineris.

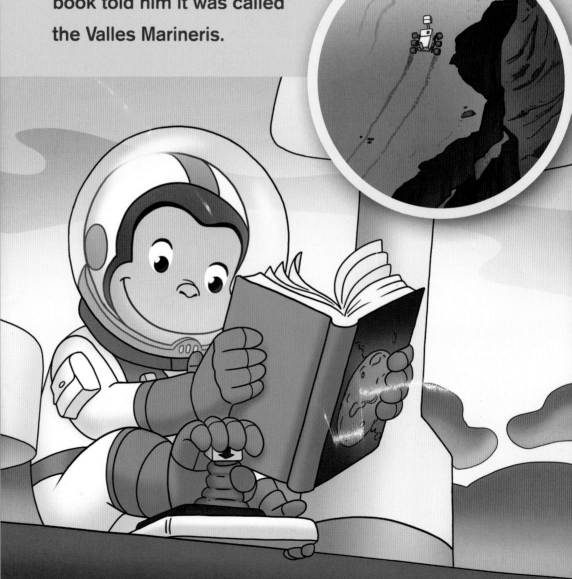

George also found the Olympus Mons, the highest volcano in our solar system. It had a great view. He wished his friend could enjoy it too.

At least George could see where his rocket had landed. He began to drive the rover back toward the spaceship.

Olympus Mons

Did you know . . .

the Olympus Mons is 16 miles (25 km) high, three times the height of Mount Everest? It is one of many volcanoes on Mars that erupted for millions of years but are no longer active.

But that's when the rover got stuck. George opened a panel and discovered great big globs of green gum were clogging up the controls! No wonder it kept sticking.

Luckily, in the low gravity of Mars, George was able to use his superstrength to pick up the vehicle and carry it back to the ship.

That was when George woke up from his dream! Now he knew why the real Mars rover was getting stuck.

Did you know . . .

that names of the Mars rovers have been Sojourner (which means "traveler"), Opportunity, Spirit, and Curiosity? Isn't Curiosity a good name for a Mars rover for George? What would you name your own Mars rover?

He led the scientists back to the control room and pointed out a gummed-up panel. Professor Einstein had been using the rover control system as a trash bin by accident! "Oops," the professor said.

Do you think the Mars rover was able to launch after all? After the control panel had been cleaned, of course!

"It's a good thing monkeys are dreamers," the man said. George agreed. He had many dreams as big as the one about traveling to Mars. Next stop: Pluto!

THERE'S MORE TO EXPLORE ABOUT THE WORLD AROUND US!

One Great Gravity Experiment

What does a cup full of water have in common with a spaceship? Find out with this experiment.

You will need . . .

- a disposable cup
- a pen or pencil to poke a hole in the cup
- water
- an outdoor area, or your bathtub

What to do:

1. With the help of an adult, poke a hole in the side of the cup.
2. Cover the hole with your thumb and fill the cup with water.
3. Hold the cup up high and uncover the hole. You'll see that the water flows out steadily. This is one reason why it's good to do this experiment outdoors or over a bathtub! Now, what do you think would happen if you let go of the cup? Would the water flow faster or slower out of the cup?
4. Cover the hole with your thumb and fill the cup with water again.
5. Hold the cup up high again, and this time, let it drop! The water stays in the cup as it falls.

What's going on? An explanation of "free fall" and "weightlessness"

When you're holding the cup, gravity pulls down on both the cup and water. But the only thing that moves is the water, because you keep the cup in place. This is the same as a spacecraft on the ground. Gravity holds the spacecraft in place, and the astronauts down on the floor. If there was a hole in the bottom of the spacecraft, the poor astronauts would fall right through, just like the water did!

It's a different story when you drop the cup. Gravity pulls down on the cup and the water equally and they fall at the same speed. The scientific term for this is free fall. This is like a spacecraft in orbit: the spacecraft and the astronauts are both constantly in free fall, and the astronauts experience weightlessness and float.

Planet Picnic

Mercury (currant)
Venus (blueberry)
Earth (raspberry)
Mars (pomegranate seed)
Jupiter (cantaloupe)
Saturn (large grapefruit)
Uranus (kiwi)
Neptune (apricot)

In order to understand how big each planet is compared to Earth, you can use fruit!

- Look in your kitchen or go to the grocery store to find one of each fruit in this chart. The chart shows the diameter of each planet divided by a billion. Diameter is the line that passes from one side of a planet to the other side.
- Line the fruits up in order and snap a picture.
- You'll notice that the last four planets are much bigger than the first four. The last four planets are called "gas giants" because their surface is made of gas. The first four planets have solid, rocky surfaces.

Planet	Diameter / billion (mm=millimeters)	Fruit stand-in
Mercury	4.9 mm	Currant or elderberry
Venus	12.1 mm	Blueberry
Earth	12.8 mm	Raspberry
Mars	6.8 mm	Pomegranate seed or raisin
Jupiter	143 mm	Cantaloupe
Saturn	120.5 mm	Large grapefruit
Uranus	51.1 mm	Kiwi or small plum
Neptune	49.5 mm	Apricot

Now comes the best part — chop your fruit up and enjoy an out-of-this-world fruit salad!

Make Your Own Constellation Viewers

The Big Upside-Down Cap—better known as the Big Dipper—is one of many constellations that are visible in the night sky. Learn the names and shapes of a few famous constellations by making your own constellation viewers!

You will need . . .

- empty toilet paper or paper towel tubes
- tinfoil
- notebook paper or tracing paper
- tape
- scissors
- a sharp pencil, safety pin, or thumbtack
- scrap cardboard or corkboard
- rubber bands

What to do:

1. Pick a constellation to view! Lay your notebook paper or tracing paper over one of the constellations on the next page and trace the template for your constellation.

2. Cut a circle around your template with your scissors and set it aside.

3. Cut a piece of tinfoil big enough to cover the end of your tube. A 4 x 4–inch square should do it.

4. Tape your constellation template to the center of the piece of tinfoil.

5. Place the foil and template on top of your cardboard or cork. Use the sharp pencil, pin, or thumbtack to poke a small hole in each dot on the template.

6. Place the foil over the end of your tube, template side in. Make sure it's centered so all of the holes are over the opening. Gently fold the extra foil around the tube and use a rubber band to hold it in place.

7. You can use markers or paint to decorate your tube. You may also want to write the name of the constellation on the side.

8. Close one eye and look through the open end of your tube with the other. Do you see your constellation? Now you can look at the stars inside, during the day, anytime! Make a few different constellation viewers and quiz your friends on which constellation is which.

Star Stories

Constellations don't just have names — they have stories, too! Learn more about some famous constellations and be sure to look for them next time you're under a starry sky.

Ursa Major, the Great Bear

Ursa Major was first spotted in the sky and named almost two thousand years ago. Many different civilizations told stories about the big bear in the sky. Do you see the Big Dipper?

Orion, the Hunter

Not all constellations are animals. Orion was named after an ancient Greek warrior. He is easy to spot by the three bright stars that make up his belt.

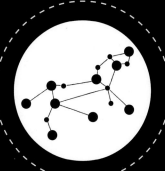

Leo, the Lion

Leo was another of the first constellations to be named, and is one of the easiest to see thanks to his crouching-lion shape. You could say Leo is king of the jungle and king of the sky!

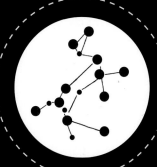

Canis Major, Big Dog

You can find Big Dog by looking for his tag: Sirius, one of the closest stars to Earth. Even if Big Dog runs away, you'll always be able to find him with the help of Sirius!

Words to Know

aquatic: living or found in water; relating to the animals and plants that live in or near water.

astronaut: a person who is trained to go to outer space.

astronomer: a scientist who studies stars, planets, and other objects in outer space.

atmosphere: the air all around us, made up of gases.

bacteria: tiny living things that exist all around you and can live inside you. Some bacteria are helpful to your body, but others can make you sick.

biology: the study of life and living things.

bitter: having a strong and often unpleasant flavor that is the opposite of sweet.

blackout: a power outage that affects a lot of people in the same area at once.

boiling point: the temperature at which a liquid begins to boil. Water's boiling point is 212 degrees Fahrenheit (100 degrees Celsius).

carbon dioxide: gas that comes from many sources, including humans or animals breathing out, which plants then take in for energy.

carnivore: an animal that eats only meat.

climate: the overall weather conditions across the seasons over long periods of time in one place.

constellation: a group of stars that forms a shape in the sky and has been given a name.

coral reef: the hard limestone skeletons left by coral polyps that build up over thousands and millions of years underwater.

cough: to force air through your throat with a short, loud noise, often because you are sick.

decompose: to break down into smaller parts.

echo: a repetition of a sound bouncing off a surface back to the listener.

echolocation: a process for finding faraway or invisible objects by bouncing sound waves off objects so that they echo back to the sender, such as a bat's screech bouncing off its prey.

ecosystem: all the living things (plants, animals, and microbes) and the nonliving parts of an environment (things like air, water, and soil), working together as a system.

electricity: a form of energy that can be found in nature or made from chemicals.

energy: the ability to do work. People get energy from food.

environment: the combination of land, weather, and living things that belong to a certain area.

equator: an imaginary line that runs around the center of the Earth and separates the Northern and Southern Hemispheres.

fertilizer: food that is added to soil to help plants grow.

force: strength or energy at work.

food chain: a system in which a plant is food for one animal, which in turn is food for another animal.

free fall: the way something falls when there is nothing pulling or holding it except for gravity.

freezing point: the temperature at which a liquid begins to freeze. Water's freezing point is 32 degrees Fahrenheit (0 degrees Celsius).

generator: a machine that makes electricity.

germ: a tiny living organism that can make you sick.

glucose: a type of sugar that is in plants and fruits and provides energy for living things, including humans.

granule: a tiny piece of material that is bigger than a grain of sand but smaller than a pebble.

gravity: the natural force that attracts things near the surface of a planet or moon and pulls them toward the surface.

Great Barrier Reef: the largest coral reef on earth—more than 1,400 miles long—off the northeastern coast of Australia.

herbivore: an animal that eats only plants.

hibernation: an inactive state in which an animal's breathing and heartbeat slow down to save energy during the winter.

ice: the solid form of water, created when the temperature drops below water's freezing point.

infect: to cause someone or something to become sick or affected by disease.

inflammation: redness, swelling, heat, and pain, usually caused by sickness or injury.

landfill: a place where garbage is buried and then covered over with soil so the land can be used for other purposes.

liftoff: the first movement of a rocket or spacecraft rising to go into space.

lungs: a pair of organs in your chest with which you breathe.

meteorologist: a scientist who studies the weather.

microscope: an instrument that magnifies very small objects and organisms so that they are large enough to be seen and studied.

migrate: to travel from one place to another, in the case of animals, because of seasonal weather changes.

mucus: a slimy fluid that coats and protects the inside of your mouth, nose, and throat.

NASA (the National Aeronautics and Space Administration): the United States government department that explores and learns more about space.

nerve: a part of a system in your body (called the nervous system) that connects to other organs and sends messages to your brain so that you can move and feel.

nocturnal: being awake at night and asleep during the day; bats and raccoons are nocturnal.

Northern Hemisphere: all of the land and water located above the equator.

nutrient: a substance or ingredient that plants, animals, and people need to live and grow. Vitamins are a type of nutrient.

oceanographer: a scientist who studies the ocean.

orbit: a circular path that one thing takes when it travels around another, such as the Earth traveling around the sun.

outer space: what exists outside of our planet Earth, including the sun and moon, other planets, stars, and more.

oxygen: a gas in the air that we need in order to breathe.

parachute: a large piece of cloth that is attached to people or things (such as a rocket) and allows them to fall slowly and land safely.

payload: the things (materials, instruments, passengers) being carried by a vehicle, such as a spacecraft.

photosynthesis: a process by which plants use the energy in sunlight to make their own food and help make oxygen for us to breathe.

planet: a large, round object in space that orbits a star. The eight planets in our solar system are Mercury, Venus, Earth, Mars, Jupiter, Saturn, Uranus, and Neptune. They all orbit the sun.

Pluto: a round object in our solar system that used to be considered the farthest planet from the sun but is now called a dwarf planet.

precipitation: rain, snow, hail, and sleet—all forms of water—that fall from the sky down to the earth.

predator: an animal that hunts other animals for food.

pruners: outdoor scissors used to trim leaves or flowers.

receptor: a nerve ending that senses changes in light, temperature, pressure, etc., and causes the body to react in a certain way.

recyclables: things that can be recycled, such as paper and glass.

recycle: to make something new out of something that has been used before.

recycling center: a place where recyclable materials are collected and sorted.

reduce: to make smaller, or less, in amount, size, or number.

reflect: to give back light, sound, or an image. A mirror reflects your face back at you.

reflex: an action of your body that happens on its own without your control or effort.

research ship: a floating science laboratory.

reuse: to use something again.

roots: the underground part of a plant that holds it in place and soaks up water from the soil.

rotation: a circular movement. The Earth rotates around the sun every 365¼ days, or one year.

saliva: the clear fluid in your mouth that helps you taste, chew, and swallow.

satellite: a machine that is sent into space and moves around the Earth, moon, sun, or a planet. Weather satellites watch the clouds and take pictures of how they move in order to gather information used to predict the weather.

savory: a pleasant flavor that is most similar to salty, without being too salty or at all sweet.

screech: a high-pitched sound, like that made by a bat.

scuba: short for self-contained underwater breathing apparatus; equipment used to breathe underwater using an oxygen tank.

seasons: four different times of year (winter, spring, summer, fall) that have their own types of weather and hours of daylight.

seed: the part of a plant that can be used to grow a new plant.

senses: sight, smell, taste, touch, and sound. These are the ways in which our body understands the world around us!

sensitive: being particularly aware of a sense, such as touch.

sensor: similar to a receptor; a part of your body that notices changes in heat, light, sound, motion, etc., and then sends the information to your brain.

shovel: a tool with a long handle that is used for moving dirt or rocks.

shuttle: an aircraft that travels between Earth and space.

sneeze: to push air out through your nose and mouth suddenly, often because you are sick.

soil: the top layer of earth in which plants grow.

solar system: the sun and everything that orbits around it. Our solar system has eight planets: Mercury, Venus, Earth, Mars, Jupiter, Saturn, Uranus, and Neptune.

sonar: a method or device for locating objects underwater by sending out sound waves.

sort: to separate into groups based on types.

Southern Hemisphere: all of the land and water located below the equator.

star: an object in space that is made of burning gas and that looks like points of light in the night sky.

submarine: a boat that travels under the water.

swim fins: flat rubber slippers used in underwater swimming. Also called flippers.

taste bud: one of the receptors on your tongue that tells you how food is flavored.

thrust: a forward push.

tone: a sound of specific quality or pitch, such as high or low.

triathlon: a three-part race usually made up of running, swimming, and biking.

trowel: a small tool with a curved blade that gardeners use to dig holes.

vitamins: natural substances usually found in foods that help your body to be healthy.

volcano: a mountain with a hole in the top that sometimes sends out melted or hot rock and steam in a sudden explosion (called an eruption).

water vapor: the gas form of liquid water, formed when water reaches its boiling point.

weather: the sunshine, wind, precipitation, and air temperature in a certain place over a short period of time.

weed: a wild plant growing where it is not wanted.

weightlessness: a feeling like floating that is experienced during free fall, when there are no outside objects touching the body or applying a push or pull to it.

wetsuit: a special suit that keeps the body warm in cold water.

Photo Credits

pp. 8, 17, 34, 35, 36, 40, 44 (top), 48 (bottom), 49, 50, 51 (kids), 52, 54, 56, 58, 62, 64, 65 (left), 66 (left), 82 (top), 97, 99, 101, 105, 115, 118 (top), 121, 129 (top), 133, 136 (bottom), 142, 148 (bottom), 157, 162, 165, 167, 173, 182, 184, 186, 187, 188, 199, 237, 246, 247, 248 (right), 249 courtesy of HMH/Carrie Garcia

p. 18 © Sharon Hoogstraten Photography/HMH

p. 24 © Eric Camden/HMH

pp. 41, 43 courtesy of HMH/Jon Whittle

pp. 48 (top), 51 (food), 65 (right), 109 (bottom) courtesy of HMH/Guy Jarvis

p. 66 (right) © Park Street Photography/HMH

pp. 69, 73, 79, 81, 82 (bottom), 85, 89, 90, 181 courtesy of HMH/Alex Mustard

p. 77 courtesy of HMH/Lazaro Ruda

p. 110 courtesy of HMH/Megan Marascalco

p. 129 (bottom) courtesy of Kevin Sawford

p. 147 courtesy of Trevor Morris

p. 148 (top) courtesy of Steve Allen

p. 159 courtesy of Phelan M. Ebenhack

p. 166 courtesy of Jody Wissing

p. 183 (background) courtesy of HMH/Victoria Smith

pp. 210, 214 courtesy of Dave Curtin

p. 219 © JPL/NASA

pp. 221, 223, 227, 229, 230, 233, 234, 239, 241, 242, 243, 244 courtesy of NASA

p. 231 courtesy of U.S. Air Force

p. 248 (background) courtesy of Jon Whittle

All other photos courtesy of Houghton Mifflin Harcourt.